Sweet
Jiminy

Sweet Jiminy

Kristin Gore

HYPERION

NEW YORK

Library of Congress Cataloging-in-Publication Data has been applied for.

ISBN: 9781401322892

Hyperion books are available for special promotions and premiums. For details contact the HarperCollins Special Markets Department in the New York office at 212-207-7528, fax 212-207-7222, or email spsales@harpercollins.com.

Design by Ralph Fowler

FIRST EDITION

10 9 8 7 6 5 4 3 2 1

SUSTAINABLE FORESTRY INITIATIVE | Certified Fiber Sourcing | www.sfiprogram.org

THIS LABEL APPLIES TO TEXT STOCK

We try to produce the most beautiful books possible, and we are also extremely concerned about the impact of our manufacturing process on the forests of the world and the environment as a whole. Accordingly, we've made sure that all of the paper we use has been certified as coming from forests that are managed, to ensure the protection of the people and wildlife dependent upon them.

My father used to tell me that there's only so much space inside a person, so you have to be careful what you let fill you up. Anger and bitterness and despair will crowd in if you let them, he said, but so will mercy and forgiveness and joy—if you make the room and invite them in. Sometimes you have to work extra hard to make the room.

His Manual for Life *advice, he called it.*

It's funny that I'm thinking about it now.

Part One

JIMINY DAVIS MISSED SLEEPING. She missed reading for pleasure and having friends and feeling confident that life held some certain purpose, but mostly, she missed sleeping. She'd always been very good at it, and she considered the fact that this skill was not valued in the corporate legal world of which she was now a part a deeply unfortunate fact. However, she was growing as accustomed to casual injustice as she was to the wincing way her thoughts now javelined through her chronically exhausted brain: both apparently came with the territory, and both gave her horrible headaches.

She knew that as a rising second-year law student she was lucky to have landed a summer associate job at a prestigious Chicago firm, yet this knowledge did nothing to alleviate a debilitating sense of panic. Because instead of feeling inspired and engaged—on the cusp of exhilarating professional opportunity—Jiminy felt listless and demoralized and utterly, prematurely, spent.

Perhaps it was this extreme exhaustion that prevented her from being seriously injured by the bike courier who slammed into her as she trudged, laden with heavy file folders and dark thoughts, through the courtyard between the firm's twin towers. Instead of tensing and shattering, her body sank inward and down like a saggy mattress, and she found herself grateful for an excuse to close her eyes. When she finally opened them, she noted that the red-faced courier was wearing a T-shirt that read "Tupelo Honey." As she stared up at it, surrounded by hundreds of billable hours of work she didn't believe in, splayed around her on the hot concrete, something deep inside her suddenly pulled up short. And she understood, instinctively, that she was done.

———

Lyn Waters had just decided to kill herself when the phone rang. It was a nightly ritual—the suicide plan, not the phone ringing—so her decision hadn't left her particularly rattled. The phone, on the other hand, had made her gasp.

"Evenin'?" she answered uncertainly.

It was definitely evening. It was the kind of syrupy summer evening that trapped minutes and held them to its pace, making it very easy to forget the time.

"It's not too late, is it, Lyn?" the anxious voice of Willa Hunt asked over the line.

"No, ma'am," Lyn answered.

At seventy-six, Lyn was five years older than Willa, but she'd been calling her "ma'am" for more than five decades. No one would have ever thought that Lyn was the least bit bothered by this. It would have been as pointless as being bothered by the moon.

"Well, I wouldn't be calling at this hour, but I just talked to Jiminy, and it sounds like she's headed this way."

For the briefest of moments, Lyn was cast backwards forty years. She brought her hand to her throat, catching her breath for the second time. But then she dropped her arm dully, feeling silly and self-indulgent. Of course Willa meant the other Jiminy.

"Isn't that nice," Lyn replied in a soothing, neutral tone, meant to calm her own inner turmoil as much as to convey the good-natured pliability Willa expected of her.

"She's getting on a bus tomorrow, so I was just hoping you could come help me get things in some kinda order."

Lyn normally only worked for Willa on Tuesdays and Thursdays. Friday was her day to tend to her own life. Still, she appreciated being needed, even if her acquiescence felt a bit compulsory.

"Well, that sounds fine. I'll see you in the mornin'," she replied.

Lyn's hand trembled a bit as she hung up the phone, another thing she should have been used to by now. As she resettled into her bed, feeling the ache of an old back injury, she thought again about her death. Every night she resolved to do herself in, and the lightness she felt once the decision was made helped her fall into a peaceful sleep. Each morning, she felt she'd had a long enough break from the world to try it anew. By noon, she'd know she'd been duped.

But for now, she closed her eyes, cradled a pillow in her arm, and willed her dreams to claim her.

———————

The nearest Greyhound bus station was a converted railroad depot thirty miles from Fayeville, Mississippi. Jiminy had been sardined against a window for sixteen hours, pinned by the girth of a woman who was unapologetic about her considerable overflow. After some initial wriggling and tentative throat clearing that produced zero response, Jiminy had resigned herself to her fate and endeavored to find something good in her predicament. Sixteen hours on a bus was never going to be a fantastic time, but there was something comforting and snug-in-the-womb-ish about not being able to move even a tiny bit. Jiminy fantasized that she was somehow gestating, and might emerge from this trial a more evolved being. How wonderful if it could be that simple.

Willa was waiting for her granddaughter at the bottom of

the bus stairs, her fleshy arms outstretched for their standard perfunctory hug.

"Are you hungry?" she asked. "Lyn's got a great supper waitin' at home, God bless her. Jiminy? You okay?"

Jiminy had gripped harder and sagged further when Willa had started to pull away. And now she was burying her face in her grandmother's shoulder, wishing she could be four years old again, when a person could burst into tears for no good reason at all.

———

Willa watched her granddaughter out of the corner of her eye as she made a careful turn off the interstate onto the access road that led to town. Jiminy had stopped crying a few miles back and was now staring straight ahead with a distant, pensive expression. Willa worried that something must have gone terribly wrong for her to come running to Fayeville, of all places. And so suddenly, away from so many more alluring plans. They hadn't seen each other in years, so for Jiminy to spontaneously visit was already strange. For her to seem so fragile was downright alarming.

Still, Willa hadn't pressed Jiminy to explain herself. She knew better than most that some things just didn't want to be talked about. In addition to its many charms and eccentricities, her tiny corner of the world was riddled with sad secrets. Had her granddaughter sensed that? Was that why she'd come— because she'd needed a place of solace to keep her own unhappy counsel?

"There's the new restaurant," Willa remarked as they cruised past its yellow painted porch. "Mexican. Can you believe it?"

Jiminy stared at the caramel-skinned young woman sweeping the pavement in front, captivated by the way her long braid was swinging in rhythm with the broom, hypnotizing passersby.

Jiminy remembered roller-skating across that same concrete as a girl, counting the cracks that rattled her teeth. Now she found herself counting again, silently, as she rolled past familiar, faded buildings. There was the old movie theater, abandoned for years, and the feed mill, and the teeny-tiny bank that looked like it could only handle toy money. There was the Comfort Inn, which had never done much business. The four hundred Fayevillians who populated the town put any guests up in their own homes. They considered the motel nice but unnecessary, like car washes or dry cleaners. They believed in handling things themselves.

As a child, Jiminy had always considered Fayeville the perfect size. There was enough to intrigue, but not overwhelm, at least as far as she knew. So she'd always felt comfortable here. Watching things slide by her now, she yearned for that feeling to again overtake her.

———————

Lyn saw the headlights approach from the kitchen window. She hated waiting for loved ones to arrive, because sometimes they never did. She passed her hand over her eyes to wipe away the pain that crept in during the day to hover there, then watched Jiminy climb out of Willa's car. She was surprised to see that she only had one bag, but seemed burdened with much more. That pale-skinned young little thing, so much more timid than her own Jiminy had been, so much more frightened of a world that rolled out a carpet for her, looked up suddenly and caught Lyn's eye. In the glow of the porch light, Jiminy's face brightened with a reflexive smile, and she stuck out her tongue and waggled it around. Despite herself, Lyn grinned back. She even chuckled. And for a split second, she felt a foreign surge of hope. Something was going to change.

J IMINY KNEW THAT she was genetically predisposed to nervous breakdowns, and had long tried to guard against them, but she worried one had crept up on her at last. She asked her grandmother as much, over breakfast her second day on the farm.

"Do I remind you of my mom? Do I seem like I'm going crazy?" she inquired anxiously.

Willa continued buttering her biscuit, and for a moment Jiminy wondered if she'd even heard. Jiminy had a tendency to speak too softly, and for all she knew, her grandmother might be going deaf as well.

But just as Jiminy was about to repeat her question more loudly, Willa cleared her throat.

"You seem like you need a good, long rest," she said. "The world's what's gone crazy. You just got old enough to notice."

Willa took a sip of her iced tea, then rose from her chair.

"So take your time," she instructed, as she placed her dishes by the sink for Lyn to clean. "Take it slow."

Jiminy watched her grandmother amble out of the kitchen toward the living room in her steady, deliberate way. And she felt comforted. Even if she was in fact on the brink of a full-scale meltdown, she didn't have to be in a rush about it. This was a relief.

———

Over the next several days, Willa and Lyn let Jiminy be for the most part—going about their regular routines, leaving her to wander the farmhouse in search of herself.

The house was more modern than many in the area—a long rectangle with large windows and a minimalist edge. Some rooms were crammed with too many things, but most felt airy and comfortable, if a bit musty. Jiminy found dead spiders and dust bunnies in most of the places she looked, but they didn't bother her. She found them reassuring actually, after the antiseptic fluorescence of the places she'd fled. She appreciated dirt and imperfection and messy signs of actual life. She didn't leave the house much—she didn't feel quite ready for that. The outside world still seemed pregnant with disappointment.

————

Willa waited patiently for her curlers to set beneath the heated helmet that she secretly feared might fry her brain if there was a freak power surge.

Every other Tuesday, Willa picked her best friend Jean up and drove the fourteen minutes into downtown Fayeville for their hair appointments. Jean herself wasn't allowed to drive since her county councilman son had confiscated her license a few months previously. Willa was still comforting Jean through this trauma. Especially out here, especially if you lived alone, not being able to drive was tantamount to house arrest. Everyone was just too spread out to get to one another easily.

Their biweekly field trip destination was Trudi's Tresses. There, Willa and Jean spent ninety minutes getting dyed, crimped, and scorched, before driving the long way back through town, talking about times past and present. Willa and Jean could glide easily from discussion of the latest store display to reminiscences about a county fair that happened thirty-five years ago. Time was a fluid plaything in their conversations.

They had so much shared history that they could happily pick and choose from it to entertain themselves for hours on end. It was simply a decision about whether to stay in the present or skip around, and they let their whims direct them.

"Any hints about how long she's gonna stay?" Jean asked.

"No," Willa replied. "As long as she likes, I suppose. I've made it clear she's welcome."

"Of course. Does Margaret know she's with you?"

Willa sighed. Her itinerant daughter was always difficult to pin down.

"I left word," Willa said. Which was often the most she could do.

"Well, I can't believe Jiminy's all grown," Jean remarked. "You remember what you were doing at her age?"

It seemed several lifetimes ago. At Jiminy's age, Willa had been a young mother, struggling to make a life on the farm with her husband Henry. By the day's standards they hadn't been well off, but they'd felt full of promise.

"Just gettin' by, I s'pose," Willa replied lightly.

"Remember our river parties?" Jean asked with a laugh.

Every Saturday night the people who farmed along the Allehany River had gathered at one or another's place and soaked up the company and relaxation that had eluded them the rest of the week. Jean and her husband Floyd had always been the life of those parties, organizing dances and stories and games. One memorable night, Floyd had hooked a dead snake to Henry's trouser leg with a fishhook and wire, then pointed out the snake with a warning yell. Henry had leapt and yelped and darted every which way to evade the rattler—everyone knew how much he despised snakes—but he of course couldn't escape. Lathered into a panic, Henry finally dove into the river. It wasn't until he noticed the uncontrollable laughter of friends who would normally be much more sympathetic that Henry caught on to the prank.

Willa smiled as she recalled this and other river gatherings, then sobered abruptly as she remembered why the parties had ceased. The river had become host to much more horrible events. She still couldn't bring herself to visit its banks, and it had been over forty years.

" 'Bout ready?" she asked Jean.

Willa herself was far from it, still stuck under her scalp fryer. She sat up straighter and felt the burn of it on her forehead, perversely grateful for the more manageable pain of the present.

———

On the grassy lawn of the courthouse square across from Trudi's Tresses, Bo Waters lay half-hidden in the shade of a hickory tree.

He was Lyn Waters's great-nephew, the grandson of her late husband's sister. Bo had left Fayeville four years previously, immediately after graduating high school, determined never to return. But now that he was done with college and studying for the MCATs, the lure of free lodging and long, slow-paced days had made him reconsider. He'd decided to come back to Fayeville for six weeks, just to study and save money, and he planned to lie low as he did both.

He'd tried reading in the tiny library catty-corner to the courthouse, but quickly found it stifling. Too many new ideas were crowding themselves into his brain, and he needed something fresher than trapped air to process them. So he'd set up camp with his books outside, in what used to be the center of town.

The stores along Main Street were all dead or dying now, mortally wounded by the opening of the monolithic HushMart Supercenter a half mile away. Bo understood he should mourn the murder of small town commerce, but at the moment he appreciated the quiet. He hadn't even minded the collection of old broken-down men sitting on the benches between the courthouse and the post office until they'd started talking.

"Reckon Trav'll throw a big to-do if his boy makes it?" one of them rasped.

"Yep, reckon he will."

"That's 'nough to get my vote. Haven't set foot on Brayer Plantation in five years, must be."

"Trav don't call it that no more. It's Brayer Farms now."

"News to me."

"S'posed to help with the colored vote or some shit."

"Shit sounds 'bout right."

Bo willed himself to continue staring at his book. Do not look up, do not give them that satisfaction, he told himself. He wasn't even sure he was denying them glee to begin with. Did they even see him here? Had those comments, that tone, been provoked by his presence, or, had he been elsewhere, would they still have landed like spittle on the parched grass browning in the sun?

This was why Bo had decided to leave Fayeville; he didn't have time for this. He sighed and tried hard to keep his attention on the diagram of the amygdala on the page in front of him as he wondered whether he was stressed enough to cause his own amygdala to jump-start his adrenal glands. There was no need to get worked up. He had to concentrate. There was a point to his studies, and distractions were only as successful as one let them be. Bo had learned to be strict with his. Forcing himself to stay calm, he focused anew.

The sound of a car horn immediately interrupted him.

"Bo Waters! Is that you?"

He looked up to see two blue-haired old ladies staring at him from the open window of a gigantic Buick. They looked like Martian poodles out for a space cruise. He blinked and registered them.

"Miz Hunt, Miz Butrell, hello," he said as he rose quickly to his feet.

He could feel the benched men staring as he crossed the grass to the waiting car. His MCAT book was heavy and unwieldy, and it made him self-conscious. He turned the cover around so it was facing his leg, away from the gaze of the women before him.

"I thought that was you," Willa said triumphantly. "I didn't know you were back. Why haven't you been to see us?"

Bo smiled politely. He liked Willa Hunt, but knew better than to indulge in any true familiarity. That same old hesitation always hooked him, even with the nicest people.

"I've just been home a couple weeks," he replied good-naturedly.

"Well I'm gonna have to take a switch to your great-aunt Lyn for not telling me so!"

Bo forced himself to smile at this. He thought he saw something flicker in Willa's eyes, perhaps remorse for her choice of phrase? It was too late regardless; her only option was to steamroll ahead. Jean Butrell seemed oblivious, content to let the two of them find their own way out of the quagmire of this already awkward conversation.

"I haven't been able to see nearly any of the people I'd like to yet," Bo said. "I gotta catch up on my catching up, I guess."

Willa smiled, a little gratefully, Bo thought. Though it could have been his imagination.

"Well, the yard's all grown up as usual, so if you wanna make a little money while you're here, just stop on by," she said graciously.

Bo did want to make a little money, but he'd budgeted his time with only the MCATs in mind.

"If I can get a break from studying, I'll be sure to head on over."

"You taking summer classes?" Willa asked. "I thought Lyn said you'd graduated."

She said this kindly, like she'd be nothing but supportive if Bo had failed to stick to the normal schooling schedule. College was a lot to take on, after all.

"I'm all done with regular classes, but I'm taking the MCAT at the end of next month in order to apply to medical school, so I've gotta buckle down for that."

"Oh!" Willa exclaimed, her mouth a perfect O of surprise.

Bo couldn't tell if she was happy to hear this or not.

"Well my, my, that *is* something'," she clucked. "Good for you."

Bo nodded, but said nothing more.

His decision to stay silent led to an uncomfortable pause, something unfamiliar on these Southern streets when ladies of a certain age and breeding were involved. Willa smiled even more widely to cover it up.

"Well, stop by and see us, ya hear?" she said.

Bo promised he would and raised his hand in goodbye. As the car pulled away, Bo could see Willa and Lyn glance at him in the rearview mirror and burst into chatter, and though an acute muscle spasm coursed through his tensed shoulder, he didn't lower his arm until they had disappeared down the road.

Jiminy scratched her shoulder absentmindedly as she skimmed another almanac. She'd discovered a pile of them in a dresser drawer in a little room at the back of the farmhouse, and had spent a delightful hour thumbing through the decades-old books, marveling at how sure they purported to be about things nobody could possibly know, such as the weather on a particular day, eleven months away. How accurate had these predictions ended up being? she wondered. Were the people who planned their lives by them idiots, or optimists, or both? And what use were the almanacs once their year had past? They became irrelevant, already proven prophetic or off-base, already gone to seed.

Jiminy liked that her grandmother kept the old almanacs around. She felt comforted to know that useless things were welcome here.

Not that Jiminy was comfortable in her uselessness. To the contrary, she longed for a purpose. She always had. Inspired at a young age by Nancy Drew and Jessica Fletcher, and later— nonfictionally—by Erin Brockovich, Jiminy had held vague ambitions of becoming a private eye or a feisty attorney. But these aspirations had taken a backseat to the day-to-day responsibilities of just getting by. Life with an unreliable mother had robbed her of the sense of security necessary for upward mobility. It had rendered her anxious and shortsighted.

When Jiminy was in college, her mother had married a wealthy retiree who delighted in her capriciousness and indulged her every whim. The two of them had taken off to travel the world, ostensibly liberating Jiminy to finally focus entirely on her own life. But the years of worry and insecurity had taken their toll, and instilled in her a reflexive skittishness that she seemed unable to shake.

It had taken all of her nerve just to move to Chicago to pursue law school, and she'd hoped this accomplishment signaled a new proactive boldness. But once there, Jiminy had continued to feel stunted and hesitant, which frustrated her. Her growing certainty that she was withholding some essential part of herself had filled her with quiet desperation. All of this had come into stark relief in the moments after she'd been taken out by the bike courier. As she'd lain there feeling for broken bones, Jiminy had been filled with revulsion for herself and her inability to fulfill the potential she surely possessed. Concerned that this disgust could harden into something crushing, she'd picked herself up, canceled her life as she knew it, and fled to the first place that popped into her mind. Had the bike courier been wearing a "Keep on Trucking" shirt, she might have ended up in San Francisco. As it was, she found herself in rural Mississippi. Exactly what she was to do now remained a mystery.

Through with the almanacs, Jiminy glanced toward the windowsill and remembered in a flash something she'd discovered about this room nineteen years before and hadn't thought of since. She ran her hands along the wood paneling beneath the window and, sure enough, felt a square portion give a little beneath her fingers. She pressed harder and experienced the same thrill she had as a six-year-old as it sprang open to reveal a secret compartment.

Peering into it, Jiminy found a translucent snail shell perched atop a book. She picked up the book and carefully dusted it off. The black leather cover was painfully cracked. It claimed to be *The Holy Bible,* but the inside pages were homemade and filled with firm, slanted handwriting that Jiminy assumed did not belong to God. The inscription on the first page confirmed this.

Henry Esau Hunt—Recollections and Resolutions

Her grandfather's name, her grandfather's writing. Her grandfather's diary? Jiminy thumbed through the roughly bound pages. The handwriting was very precise, but faded and difficult to read. The first entry was dated January 1, 1954, and titled "Our Wedding Day."

It contained a brief description of the event, really just a record of the fact that Henry Esau Hunt had married Willa Calamity Peal in the presence of their parents and a minister at noon on that New Year's Day. The entry seemed dispassionate enough, though Jiminy supposed it had meant enough to Henry to warrant beginning this book.

From that day forward, it appeared that Henry had made an entry every six months or so, only to record a happening deemed significant. As the years wore on, he began adding slightly to the entries—just bare-boned commentary that hinted at what he might have been feeling at the time. On January 6, 1959, Henry noted that Margaret Peal Hunt was born at eight thirty-five in the morning. Henry had written: "A long, hard night. A joyous day." Jiminy smiled ruefully, reflecting that her mother continued to be known for such extremes.

She flipped to the last entry, which occurred about two-thirds of the way through the book, with plenty of blank pages left to be filled. It was dated January 1, 1967, and it read: "Hard year, hopeless. Poor Lyn, poor us." And then, nothing more.

Jiminy knew that her grandfather had died suddenly and unexpectedly when her mother was eight years old. She was less certain that he'd been killed by a lost tribe of Indians hiding in the surrounding hills, or a roving band of land pirates, or a swarm of killer vampire bats up from the Louisiana swamps. All of these explanations had been offered to Jiminy by her mother, with considerable flourishes, but Jiminy had instead accepted a cousin's report that her mother's father had succumbed to a massive, sudden pulmonary embolism, and died very prematurely at the age of thirty-two, leaving his wife and daughter to fend for themselves as best they could.

Since Jiminy's mother had been born in 1959, she would have turned eight years old in 1967, the year of Henry's final entry. It seemed he'd died before he could make another one. Had the hardness and hopelessness he'd written about brought on the embolism? Was that just a medical term for an unfixable broken heart?

Poor Lyn, poor us. Jiminy assumed the Lyn he referred to was the Lyn she knew. The Lyn who had worked for her grandmother for over fifty years, and in whose indifferent disregard Jiminy had always found a special solace. The most anyone could hope for from Lyn was a gruff affection that could be easily mistaken for dislike. Still, Jiminy had always gravitated toward her, because as shy as Jiminy was, there was something about Lyn that drew her out. Now that she thought about it, Jiminy felt an intense gratitude for Lyn that she'd never adequately expressed. Why hadn't she? She decided she would. That was something she could do.

Poor Lyn, poor us. What had happened to Lyn? What had happened to all of them?

Jiminy moved backwards through the pages, looking for answers. Her hand paused on an entry that read: "Edward and Jiminy found, buried. Awful."

For a moment, she felt like she couldn't breathe, like she'd stumbled across a hidden portal into the future and was illicitly reading about her own demise. She'd been found and buried, but how had she died? She shivered. The date of the entry was June 24, 1966. There had obviously been another Jiminy. She'd never in her entire life heard of her, not even in her mother's crazier stories. Who was she?

"Scarin' up the devil in here?"

Jiminy leapt up, slamming the book shut as she whirled around in surprise. Lyn was standing in the doorway, her shoulders stooped with age. She was taken aback by Jiminy's sudden fright. It made her clutch her own heart in solidarity.

"Lord child, what's wrong with you?"

"Sorry," Jiminy replied, somewhat breathlessly.

She wondered if Lyn recognized the book clasped in her hands. Lyn was looking at her strangely.

"Your grandma just wanted to make sure you were still alive since we hadn't heard a peep outta you all mornin'," Lyn said flatly, before turning to leave.

Jiminy stared after her, stricken. She wanted to stop her. She had things to say. She had things to ask.

"Wait," she said, but it came out a whisper that Lyn didn't appear to hear.

"Wait," Jiminy repeated. "Thank you."

She'd meant to say this loudly, and meaningfully, but again the words barely escaped her throat, and they drifted ineffectually toward Lyn's hunched, retreating back, too weak to possibly be heard.

B O WATERS'S BACK HURT from pushing a lawnmower over Willa Hunt's endless yard. When he had done this chore for her years ago, there'd been a tractor-mower he could sit and ride on, turning the task into a relatively painless journey in the hot sun. But now he was stuck with some contraption from the last century, without an engine in sight. It was a hand-powered rotary mower meant for a much smaller lawn than Willa's. Bo was sweating and grunting, and not even done with a sixth of his task. He'd better get paid considerably more for this. He tried to succumb to the rough pleasure of physical exertion—he'd been a decent athlete in high school but hadn't done much since. It occurred to him that perhaps this was his first step back into shape; that maybe he should be grateful for the immense inconvenience of this stupid machine.

As he was distracting himself from his throbbing muscles by cursing the lawn mower, Bo was suddenly stopped by a timid sneeze. He looked toward the sound and saw a movement by the woodpile. Expecting a cat or a groundhog, Bo was startled to see a human form rise slowly from the other side. A female human form.

"Hi," Jiminy said, sneezing again.

"Hi," Bo replied, aware of the pollens floating in the air between them. He wondered how many of his curses had been overheard.

"I'm allergic to grass," Jiminy said, by way of explanation.

"That's a tough one to avoid," Bo replied.

Didn't Jiminy know it. She was allergic to dust also, and

wheat, and easy human interaction, or at least it frequently seemed so to her.

"Do I know you? You look familiar," she said, with her head cocked to the side in an inquisitive way that didn't feel totally natural to her, but that she hoped was fitting for the moment. Her neck hurt from how she'd been sitting against the wood-pile.

"You do, too," Bo replied. "I'm kin to Lyn. I'm Bo."

"I'm Jiminy. Willa's my grandmother."

They'd made their introductions, declared their affiliations. Jiminy stood waiting for some inspiration about how to continue this conversation. She wanted it to go forward, she liked the look of this guy. It wasn't just that he was the first person younger than seventy that she'd encountered in the past week, though that probably was part of the attraction. But there was more. He had a smooth assurance to his features that made Jiminy feel calm.

"How old are you?" she blurted.

Bo stared back at her.

"Twenty-one," he replied. "Is that old enough?"

Jiminy blushed.

"I guess so," she replied. "Except for renting cars."

"Who needs a rental car when I've got these hot wheels?" Bo replied, lifting up the lawn mower he longed to fling into the nearby river.

Jiminy laughed.

"Are you doing the whole lawn?" she asked.

Bo nodded wearily.

"I should be finished in a couple months. Do you know what happened to your grandmother's tractor-mower? I'll pay you a thousand dollars if you tell me where it is."

Jiminy laughed again.

"Sorry, I don't know where much of anything is. I haven't been here in years."

"What brings you back?"

Jiminy looked down, unsure of how to answer. Could she say she was running away? Should she tell Bo about her restlessness, and desperation, and how her unsatisfactory world had abruptly folded in on her? Should she mention her mother, and her nervous breakdown destiny? Or admit how random it was that she'd chosen this spot for refuge? She opened her mouth to let all of this out, then closed it again.

"Just getting a break from city life," she managed to say at last.

Bo nodded, unperturbed by Jiminy's awkwardness. He could tell she had plenty more to say, but he felt no urge to pry. Like anyone who wasn't actually from here, Jiminy assumed Fayeville represented a relaxing respite from busier places, but Bo knew there was as much turmoil here as anywhere. If she stuck around, she'd find that out for herself.

"How long you staying?" he asked.

"Just taking it day by day," she answered with a shrug. "How are you related to Lyn?"

"She's my great-aunt. I lived with her some growing up."

Jiminy glanced down at the book in her hand, then snapped her gaze back up to meet Bo's.

"Do you happen to know . . . I mean, I guess you probably would . . . but maybe not, who knows how much families communicate . . . Um, was Lyn ever married, by any chance?"

Bo felt sorry for Jiminy that she had to expend so much effort to ask a simple question. What a difficult way to go through life. He had his challenges, but most of them felt imposed from the outside, not created within. And now Jiminy was looking at him fearfully, like she was worried she'd overstepped her bounds somehow.

"Aunt Lyn was married to my grandma's brother, Edward Waters. And they had a daughter, but she died. He died, too— both a long time ago. Aunt Lyn never hooked up with anyone else, as far as I know."

Jiminy nodded.

"She doesn't talk about it," Bo continued. "No one else does either, to keep from upsetting her. What I know, I heard from a drunk old uncle talking outta school."

Jiminy nodded again. She considered showing Bo her grand-father's diary, but decided to keep it to herself for the time being.

"Is that a Polaroid camera?" Bo asked.

He was pointing to the camera dangling from her neck. Jiminy had brought it with her from Chicago, to document her decline. She touched it now, and nodded.

"I didn't even know they made them anymore," Bo remarked. "I used to love those things. Such instant gratification."

Jiminy nodded again, in complete agreement. She resisted the urge to snap a photo of Bo right that second.

"So what do people do for fun around here?" she asked in-stead.

"Oh, we go cow-tipping, throw crab apples at the Hardee's billboard, make crank calls," Bo answered.

Jiminy tried to imagine herself doing these things with any amount of enthusiasm. Maybe the crab apple thing, if she ac-tually managed to hit the billboard.

"I'm kidding," Bo continued. "We're not that bad off. Though I have been known to spend rainy days in the sports aisle of HushMart. You can get a pretty good basketball game going before they ask you to move on."

"I'm the queen of HORSE," Jiminy replied.

It was true. She wasn't athletic in general, but she had a preternatural talent for making basketball shots. Not while on the move, and she couldn't dribble or pass or be sure of many rules of the game, but she could get that ball through the hoop from practically any standing position, no matter the distance.

"The queen, huh?" Bo replied.

His tone wasn't skeptical; it was more amused. Still, Jiminy found herself resenting it. She wasn't good at many things. She felt she proved this nearly every day.

"I'm not kidding," she insisted, with uncharacteristic fire. "I've never lost a game. I've never been anything more than a HOR."

Bo raised his eyebrows.

"H-O-R," she clarified, feeling her face flush.

Bo grinned and put his hands up in surrender.

"Do you coach lesser players?" he asked.

"Anytime," Jiminy answered, surprised at her confidence.

"I'm gonna come find you when I finish this," Bo said, motioning to the vast expanse of unmown lawn around him. "If I live that long."

Jiminy smiled, happy to realize she still could.

———

Inside, Lyn had been watching them through the window for the past ten minutes, thinking about when they'd first met as children. She doubted either one of them remembered it.

Jiminy had been only six years old, dropped off by her quarreling parents for an impromptu visit. She was a silent, reserved child, and she'd quickly become Lyn's little shadow, sitting for hours on the stool in the corner the kitchen, shyly watching her every move. Lyn had gone about her business as usual, but every once in a while she'd stuck out her tongue without warning and waggled it around, causing Jiminy to erupt into paroxysms of giggles. Just as suddenly, Lyn would resume her poker face and reabsorb herself in her task. Jiminy would giggle a little longer to herself, then wait patiently for the next show.

That was also the trip that Jiminy had taken to drinking buttermilk. Lyn had never known a child to actually enjoy the taste. She watched Jiminy first sip some by accident, assuming it was regular milk. Lyn had waited for her grimace, but the girl simply cocked her head in surprise and took a longer sip. Not realizing that she wasn't supposed to like it, she'd started drinking it regularly.

Lyn had been watching little Jiminy pour herself another tall glass of buttermilk, and wondering if there'd be enough left for the biscuits she was supposed to make, when an unfamiliar car turned down the long gravel lane. The sight of a strange vehicle made Lyn anxious, and she reflexively reached for the big butcher knife, not entirely sure what she planned to do with it. Lyn was relieved when she recognized her late husband's niece climbing out of the car. She watched her unstrap a toddler from the backseat—a toddler whom Lyn had previously only heard jabbering and squealing in the background of a phone conversation. A toddler who turned out to look very much like her beloved Edward: the same eyes, those same steady features. The kind of face you wanted to drink up to calm yourself down. Lyn loved Bo as soon as she saw him, even from that distance; even through a window that needed cleaning.

She had hurried out the kitchen door, wondering whether Willa would mind this unexpected visit, considering she wasn't particularly partial to children or interruptions. But to Lyn's relief, Willa had looked up from the science labs she'd been grading on the porch and calmly introduced herself to Edward's niece and her toddler. And then Jiminy had appeared, glass of buttermilk in hand.

"Who's that?" she asked, pointing her little finger at him.

"His name is Bo, Jiminy," Willa said.

Edward's niece had flashed a look Lyn's way, which Lyn ignored. Yes, the girl was named Jiminy. No, Lyn didn't want to talk about it.

"Oh," Jiminy said. "Would he like some buttermilk?"

And she had sat down beside Bo on the grass in the sun. She tried to teach him patty-cake. Bo laughed and grabbed at her fingers and made her shriek. Lyn hadn't known how to feel, watching them. She'd looked to Willa to break them up, or let them play. But Willa had returned to grading her papers, forfeiting her prerogative to pass judgment.

Edward's niece hadn't stayed long—not at Willa's farm, not even in Fayeville. She'd already decided that her destiny lay elsewhere, and no amount of disappointment could sway her from its pursuit. No amount of responsibility, either. She simply shrugged it off, the way happiness had shrugged her.

Bo, on the other hand, had remained right there in Fayeville from then on, passed around from relative to relative, looked after by the group of them. His mother and grandmother had kept "Waters" as their last name, instead of giving any credence to the men who had dipped into and out of their lives, so Bo blended right in with the family. But he and Jiminy had never crossed paths again. Jiminy had traveled from her home in southern Illinois to visit Willa a few more times, but Lyn hadn't had charge of Bo during those visits. And then Jiminy had stopped coming altogether once she'd become preoccupied with trying to be an adult.

But here she was now, walking into the kitchen, all grown. Lyn handed her a glass of buttermilk that she'd absentmind-edly poured as she'd reminisced. Jiminy looked understand-ably confused. Realizing what she'd done, Lyn almost snatched the glass back, but Jiminy was already raising it to her lips.

"Thanks," she said quizzically, taking a sip.

Just as she had when she was a child, she drank with her eyes wide open. And she still didn't wince at the sourness.

Two hours later, as Lyn sat folding pillowcases by the window, she watched Bo cross the freshly mown lawn to the house. She heard him let himself in the front door, cross the entryway, and knock on Jiminy's door. Lyn stayed in the kitchen, quiet and still.

"Sorry, didn't mean to interrupt," she heard Bo say.

"I'm glad you did," Jiminy answered, so light and free.

"Have you recovered from your allergy attack?"

"Nearly."

"Well, I got revenge for you," Bo assured. "That grass won't be bothering anyone for a while."

"Thanks, I owe you one. Are you taking off now?"

"I was gonna go see a superstore about a HORSE. Wanna come?"

"Definitely," Jiminy replied.

Lyn heard them make their way to the door, where they must have run into an unsuspecting Willa.

"What's going on? Is everything okay?" she heard Willa ex-claim, her voice mildly alarmed.

"Everything's fine," Jiminy replied. "I'm headed into town with Bo."

"Oh," Willa answered.

And Lyn knew the exact O her mouth was making.

"Do you need anything?" Jiminy asked.

"I don't know," Willa replied uncertainly. "I don't suppose so."

"Okay, see you later then!" Jiminy replied sunnily.

Then the door closed, and Lyn heard Willa sigh deeply.

"Shit," Willa said, thinking she was saying it to herself.

In the other room, Lyn closed her eyes and slowly shook her head.

A few weeks later, Willa sat anxiously by the kitchen window, shuffling Jiminy's stack of Polaroids and peering out into the darkness every few minutes. Willa had been surprised that Jiminy just left her photos around for anyone to look at, for anyone to judge. She flipped through them again, quickly enough that she created a moving picture of her granddaughter's last few weeks—a cascading waterfall of captured moments.

There was Bo holding a basketball at HushMart, and Bo pointing to a diagram of the human heart with a mock-serious expression, and Bo lying on his back in the field behind the barn. There were a lot of Bo. There were a few of Willa, too—looking up from her crossword with a questioning expression, coming in the door with an armful of azaleas, sitting in her porch chair smiling. And there was Lyn baking biscuits, and carrying a stack of towels, and gazing out the kitchen window. But mainly the Polaroids were of Bo. Willa looked up from them and out into the night again, willing headlights to appear.

She hadn't waited up for someone to come home since her daughter was a teenager, and she felt out of practice. And a little ridiculous. First of all, waiting for her daughter hadn't ever kept her out of trouble, nor had it forged the meaningful, long-term relationship Willa had always assumed she'd enjoy with her offspring. Secondly, and more to the present point, her granddaughter was twenty-five and therefore didn't have a curfew. But she was a young, uncertain twenty-five, spending time in a place she didn't understand, and Willa felt apprehensive. Jiminy and Bo had been thick as thieves lately, but they generally called it a night at a decent hour. It was now nearly eleven. What could they be doing?

She dialed Lyn, who answered the phone sounding surprised.

"Lyn, it's Willa. Have you heard from Bo?"

"No, ma'am. What's the matter? What's happened?"

Willa felt guilty for introducing that note of panic into Lyn's night. But at least she wouldn't be the only one worrying now.

"Nothing, it's just Jiminy's not back yet and it's getting late. You don't know where they went?"

"Bo's staying at his friend's this summer, not with me. And he's grown now, so I don't ask too many questions."

Willa knew this was a reasonable position, but still, it angered her.

Lyn waited for Willa to say something more. She could feel the tension on the line; could sense that she was being blamed for Jiminy's whereabouts. And though she liked that odd little girl just fine, there was only one Jiminy she'd ever wanted to be responsible for, and that Jiminy had been taken from her. She didn't have the energy for another, even if she was Willa's granddaughter.

She heard Willa suck her breath in between her teeth. It sounded chilly and impersonal, the whistle of an ill wind. When she spoke again, her voice was tight and controlled.

"Bo's not into any bad news now, is he?"

There was none of the loose warmth that Willa's vowels normally slid around in—they seemed mired in something cold and congealed.

Lyn took a moment to reply. Was Bo into any bad news? Of his own accord? More than the everyday bad news he had to swallow and shoulder and wade through and wear down? Nothing more than that. No, Bo wasn't into any bad news. Not the kind Willa was intimating. Lyn kept her calm.

"No, ma'am, he sure isn't. He's studying for the imp-cats, you know."

"The MCATs," Willa corrected testily.

Willa knew Lyn knew all about the MCATs. Knew she wasn't actually correcting her, but merely pointing out the slight speech impediment that crept into Lyn's pronunciations when she got agitated. Which was rare—Lyn was usually too disengaged to get at all riled, so her speech stayed steady. Willa felt cruel for having caused the distress, and petty for mocking its consequences.

"Yes, ma'am. Imp-cats. M . . . CATs," Lyn said.

"I just didn't expect them to spend so much time together," Willa continued.

She was trying to explain, but was only making it worse.

"Mmm-huh" was the reply.

"Well, I'm sure she'll be back soon. Will we be seeing you Thursday?"

"Mmm-huh."

Willa walked herself around the kitchen to try and straighten herself out. She'd offended Lyn, she knew, and she'd confused herself even further. What could she do to make it up? Maybe a yellowcake. Lyn always loved yellowcake.

She'd just cracked an egg and shaken away the unpleasant memory of cracking a fertilized one years ago—oh, the unwelcome surprise of embryonic development when all you wanted was breakfast—when she saw the headlights turn into the drive.

———————

Jiminy felt like a better version of herself around Bo. She was less shy, less nervous, more curious, more lively. She hoped he'd been enjoying himself, too, and that she was more than just a mildly entertaining diversion from dry medical texts. But they hadn't discussed how they felt. They hadn't had physical contact besides friendly shoulder squeezes and high fives on the makeshift basketball court. Which was appropriate, Jiminy knew, at least where Fayeville was concerned. Anything more than a friendship would be frowned upon—even still, even today. Even so, Jiminy had let herself imagine a romance, and recognized that anticipating the disapproval it would engender actually made it that much more tempting to her. She was annoyed at herself for this—for harboring impure motivations. She believed she should want something solely for the thing itself, not because it was surprising or controversial. Because she was falling short, she felt as tainted as the town, and this shielded her from delusions of moral superiority.

Jiminy wasn't thinking about any of this at the moment, however. She couldn't think of anything besides what she'd just experienced. In fact, she wasn't positive she'd ever be able to think about anything else again.

At her cajoling, Bo had taken her to visit the crazy old great-uncle who'd talked of his aunt Lyn's past when no one else would. Bo's Uncle Fred lived on a hilltop two counties over, forty minutes away, and he'd proven as loquacious as advertised.

"If it isn't Mr. Bojangles!" he exclaimed as they pulled up to his sprawling, chaotic abode.

There was a house amid the clutter, but you had to look hard for it. A tree was growing through Fred's front porch, and a couch and coffee table sat in the yard. There was an inside-out feeling to the whole place, as if it had been scooped up by a tornado, churned around, and spat back out in no particular order. Plants, animals, and furniture spilled all over one another. It was almost a caricature of a backwoods eccentric's lair.

"And who've ya brung?" Fred bellowed. "Who've ya brung with ya, Mr. Bojangles?"

"Hey, Uncle Fred. This is my friend Jiminy," Bo answered.

Fred had rushed toward them, surprisingly fast for a man so frail and gnarled, and peered intently at Jiminy's face.

"There's only one Jiminy," he said finally. "You must be someone else."

Jiminy had been holding her breath without realizing it. She exhaled then, keeping her gaze steady. Fred's eyes were rheumy but bright.

"I must be," she agreed.

And then the three of them had sat in Fred's outdoor living room, surrounded by strutting peacocks, and talked for hours.

Now, as the car rolled slowly homeward, Jiminy's head was stuffed with more of a story than she knew what to do with. She felt it pressing against the back of her eyes and welling up in her throat, threatening to overwhelm her.

"You okay?" Bo asked.

Jiminy considered. What a question, given what they now knew. How could she be, really? How could anyone? She could still hear Fred's words echoing in her head.

"They hunted 'em," he'd said. "They hunted Jiminy and Edward and they got 'em. Ran Edward's car off the road and drug 'em out and shot 'em. Threw 'em in the river, burned their car. Don't know who exactly—thing is, it coulda been any of 'em. It coulda been all of 'em. That's the way things were."

Listening to Fred, Jiminy had cried long, stringy tears and felt herself unraveling.

"But why?" she'd asked.

Fred picked some mites off a peacock chick while he let the question hang. It took a full minute of silence before Jiminy had understood its significance and regretted her question. There was no attaching rationality to such a thing. Darkness knew no bounds.

As they were saying their goodbyes a little later, Fred had offered Jiminy a handkerchief.

"She shone too bright is why," he said, before ducking back into his falling-down, inside-out home.

Jiminy pondered this now, twisting Fred's handkerchief between her fingers. She didn't realize that she was shaking.

"J?" Bo asked, lightly touching her arm. "You okay?"

She pulled herself together.

"As okay as possible," she replied.

Bo nodded, looking older than he ever had. He turned off the road into Willa's long driveway, careful to slow down for the gravel.

"You need any more company?" he asked quietly, as he pulled up to the house.

Through the window that looked like it needed cleaning, Jiminy could see her grandmother in the kitchen and was struck by how powerfully she resembled her mother.

"I'll be all right," she replied, as she climbed from the car.

She was already out before it occurred to her how selfish her shock had made her. Bo had more reason to be upset, after all. She bent her knees and leaned into the open window.

"Oh God, what about you?" she asked, her voice full of concern.

Bo smiled a smile that seemed more a part of the frown genre.

"I'm okay," he said.

Jiminy was unconvinced.

"Really, I'm okay," Bo repeated, making an effort to sound more reassuring. "I'm good."

Jiminy sighed. Whatever their emotional state, she agreed that he was. Which was saying something, in this world.

———

Willa wiped some flour off her arm and tried to compose her face into a mellow arrangement, away from its mask of worry.

"Hi," Jiminy said, as she walked into the kitchen.

"Oh, hello," Willa replied pleasantly. "I couldn't sleep, so I decided to make a yellowcake. It's Lyn's favorite."

Jiminy nodded, but Willa felt like her granddaughter was staring right through her, out somewhere behind her body, beyond these walls.

After a long moment, Jiminy focused her saucer eyes back on her grandmother's.

"Tell me about Edward and Jiminy," she commanded.

Willa felt a tightening in her chest, and reached behind her for the counter edge to sink against.

————————

Jiminy was waiting for Lyn when she pulled into the drive Thursday morning. Waiting outside, sitting on the stump of the oak tree that a storm had taken down two summers ago. Willa had planned to get it removed before observing that it made a convenient chair. For shucking corn or snapping beans or just letting the breeze soothe some of your day, Lyn thought, as she climbed slowly out of her car. Not for someone looking to bother her before she'd had her coffee.

"Get any worms?" Lyn asked, as Jiminy jumped up and moved toward her.

Jiminy looked confused. Lyn didn't feel like explaining her early bird joke, even when Jiminy began looking behind her and nervously dusting off the seat of her jeans.

"Did you talk to Bo?" Jiminy asked.

Was that what this was about? Lyn wondered. She didn't think it had gotten to that stage yet with these two, though it was surely headed there, if someone didn't intervene. Whether Lyn or anyone else liked it, she could see it hovering, waiting to be.

"Not about anything special," Lyn answered.

"Well, can I talk to you?" Jiminy asked.

Lyn looked at her expectantly.

"You may not want to discuss this and I may be out of line," Jiminy continued a bit breathlessly. "But I heard something that I want to ask you about."

"Shoot," Lyn said, and wondered why the girl winced.

Jiminy took a deep breath.

"I heard about what happened to your husband and daughter," she said.

It was Lyn's turn to breathe deep. Here was the abyss, suddenly at her doorstep.

"I heard how they went missing, and how they turned up killed," Jiminy continued. "And I am so sorry. I don't know the words to say how sorry."

Lyn didn't say anything back. She sank down onto the stump Jiminy had vacated, setting the paper bag of potatoes she'd brought with her on the ground and letting her purse slide down her arm to keep it company.

"She had my name," Jiminy blurted.

"You have hers," Lyn replied quietly.

"Right, of course, I have hers. I didn't mean . . . My mother knew her?"

"Your mother worshiped her."

"How uh . . . how old was she when she passed?"

Bo's great-uncle hadn't been completely sure. He'd said around fifteen. Willa had said nearly eighteen, though she really hadn't wanted to say much about it at all.

"She didn't 'pass,' she was shot in the head and thrown in the river," Lyn said evenly. "There was nothin' gentle or natural about it."

Jiminy kept her eyes trained on the ground, but Lyn saw they were leaking tears.

"She was seventeen," Lyn continued. "Smarter than all getout. What I lived and breathed for."

Besides Edward, Lyn added in her head. She'd lived and breathed for him, too.

"And your husband . . . ?" Jiminy asked.

"Edward was shot in the back. Thrown in the river, too."

They weren't very good swimmers, not that it would have mattered by that point. Still, it was something that had tormented Lyn, the thought of their souls trying to leave their bodies and not knowing how to swim to the surface. She had to imagine they'd left earlier. She had to imagine that, or she'd go insane.

"Do you know who did it?" Jiminy asked softly.

The only answer that would make any sense to her was some demon up from the underworld, something that sucked and snorted pure evil.

Lyn was shaking her head. Which is what Willa had done, and Bo's uncle before her.

"They really never caught them?" Jiminy asked incredulously.

Lyn raised her gaze to meet hers.

"You act like they even tried."

JIMINY BEGAN SNEEZING immediately upon entering the Fayeville Public Library. There were no other patrons inside the tiny two-room building to object, but the librarian behind the counter looked startled.

"May I help you?" she croaked.

Jiminy wondered if she was the first person to whom the librarian had spoken all day.

"Yes, thank you," Jiminy replied, sneezing again. "Sorry, I'm allergic to dust."

The librarian looked offended. Jiminy forged ahead.

"I'm trying to find information on something that happened in Fayeville in June of 1966. Do you have newspapers from that year?"

The librarian blinked once, twice, three times. Jiminy wondered if this was some physical manifestation of her mental process. Maybe she was flipping through options in her brain, clicking them forward with her eyelids like an old-fashioned slide show. Finally, she spoke.

"Nothing besides the *Fayeville Ledger*. You gotta head to the big city library for the big city papers."

And the fast-talking, big city gals, Jiminy added to herself. The librarian didn't seem to be using these terms with any sense of humor, but they struck Jiminy as fake, like they'd been written in a script to be used when outsiders came a-callin'.

Was she an outsider? Jiminy felt connected to this town through her family, though she'd really only spent a little over four months of her life here, all totaled up. She'd been raised elsewhere—not too far away, but definitely elsewhere. Her mother hadn't ever wanted to come back to Fayeville, even before her breakdown.

"I'm Willa Hunt's granddaughter," Jiminy offered, to prove that she wasn't completely out of place here. She felt it was important to make that known.

Sure enough, the librarian softened.

"Your grandma's a good woman," she said. "Taught me biology, matter a fact."

Jiminy knew that Willa had been a schoolteacher, but she still had trouble picturing it.

"She encouraged me to be a doctor, actually," the librarian continued. "Said there was no reason a woman shouldn't be. Said she'd always dreamed of being one herself, but it wasn't meant to be."

This was a surprise to Jiminy. She'd never thought of her grandmother as someone who harbored unfulfilled dreams.

"You said June 1966?" the librarian queried.

Jiminy nodded, realizing she'd been mutely preoccupied with her inner monologue. Her tendency to do this didn't do wonders for her social interactive skills. She goosed herself to speak.

"I'm looking for any write-ups about something that happened that month. A couple of murders," Jiminy replied.

"Well that woulda been front page news, so it should be easy to find," the librarian answered. "I don't remember hearing about anything like that though. You sure you got your facts right?"

Jiminy nodded.

"All right, the old papers are over there."

The librarian directed Jiminy to the *Fayeville Ledger* archives, which consisted of a stack of cardboard boxes filled with yellowed newspapers in various stages of decomposition. Jiminy found the "1966–68" box and sneezed her way through to June. Since the *Ledger* was published biweekly, there were only two thin copies from that month, and neither had any mention of Edward and Jiminy Waters.

There was an opinion piece that caught her eye, though. It was titled "Coon Season" and it was written by Travis Brayer. She assumed he was related to Bobby Brayer, who was currently running for governor. The Brayer family owned a huge old cotton plantation just outside Fayeville. Jiminy didn't pay much attention to politics, but a person couldn't help but notice the billboard at the edge of town that read, "Fayeville: Proud Home of State Senator Bobby Brayer." Several "Brayer for Governor" signs had colonized the patch of grass beneath it, along with most of the yards in town.

According to Travis Brayer's article, he was upset about the "Negro uprising" happening in a neighboring state and felt compelled to warn the citizens of Fayeville that such dangerous unrest could spread to their own backyard if they didn't stand guard and tamp it down. He made reference to "that uppity Meredith boy" and urged his fellow townspeople to stay vigilant.

Jiminy closed her eyes and tried to remember what she could about the Meredith Marches of 1966. She knew they had something to do with desegregation, something to do with voting, something to do with Martin Luther King, Jr. Unable to come up with anything more, she opened her eyes and looked around for a computer, but there was none to be found. Fayeville's dearth of Internet connections was simultaneously charming and inconvenient. Jiminy reached for the encyclopedia set on a nearby shelf, feeling very old-fashioned.

Forty minutes later, she better understood that the summer of 1966 had been one of inflamed passions, of galvanization and conflict, of the South near its boiling point. This apparently had made for a place and time when innocent people could be slaughtered and forgotten. But really? Could they really?

She checked the July issues of the paper, and the August and September ones, just to be sure. There was no mention anywhere.

"Find what you're looking for?" the librarian asked between bites of the salad she'd brought for her lunch.

Jiminy shook her head.

"No, actually. There were two brutal murders of people who lived right here in Fayeville, and there's not a single mention of them anywhere."

"You must have your dates wrong," the librarian replied. "You can check the 1965 box if you like."

"It was 1966. Lyn Waters's husband and daughter, Edward and Jiminy, were murdered that June. They were driving back from a leadership seminar Jiminy had won an essay contest to attend and they went missing. Two weeks later their car was found stripped and burned on the banks of the river. Their bodies washed ashore nearby."

The librarian's expression changed as Jiminy recited these facts. She put down her fork.

"Those aren't the sort of deaths the *Ledger* covered back then," she said evenly.

"Do you remember hearing about them?" Jiminy asked.

The librarian met her gaze.

"I remember hearing that Lyn's husband and daughter had gone and got themselves drowned. I didn't ask any questions. We don't talk about things like that."

Jiminy stared back, then sneezed powerfully, grateful that her body instinctively rejected such attitudes. Unfortunately this town seemed rife with them, and she was beginning to feel allergic to simply being here.

She took her leave and exited into the bright sunshine of the courthouse yard, where, slightly dazed, she made her way to the nearest tree and sank into its shade. With one hand on her diaphragm and the other propped beneath her head, she lay on her back, closed her eyes, and focused on her breath. She began to count how many heartbeats she could fit into one inhalation and had just stretched herself to three when she sensed someone standing over her. Her heartbeat surged as her eyes flew open. It was Bo.

"You looked so peaceful," he said.

"It's a good disguise," she answered.

His grin was easily unfurled. She gazed at his white, white teeth and thought of sails on Lake Michigan.

"Do you wanna go get some food or something?" she asked.

It wasn't like her to usher an invitation, but she'd come to realize that spending time with Bo delighted her. Her life had been short on delight and she felt greedy for it now.

Bo's grin tacked starboard as he shook his head.

"I'd love to, but I haven't earned it yet," he answered. "I've got a long date with the lymphatic system," he said as he held up his MCAT book. "Maybe later?"

"Lymph node hussies," Jiminy muttered.

Bo laughed.

"You sticking around?" he asked. "This is my favorite spot to study."

Jiminy thought about it.

"No, I've got things to do, too," she replied. "But call me later?"

"Will do."

His promise flapped in the air between them, crisp and clear and healthy.

WHENEVER WILLA walked into the HushMart superstore, she felt like she was arriving in another country and should have to show her passport for entry. An entire populace could live in the building and have everything they needed at their fingertips, at low, low prices. It was a wonder of a place.

She still occasionally happened upon entire sections that seemed new to her, and she wondered if the store was secretly expanding at night. The lot that had been zoned for it backed up to a limestone cliff, so there wasn't anywhere obvious for it to grow, but Willa had a hunch that those light green–vested managers were far too innovative to let a little geology hamper their progress.

"Have you sampled our hickory-smoked chew toys?" a voice chirped.

It was one of the green-vests, offering what appeared to be a barbecue-scented shoe.

"No, thank you," Willa replied.

"They're for dogs. Do you have a dog?"

Willa shook her head.

"Then you're in luck! The store's opening a pet zone next month, so you can buy one!"

"Buy one? Fayeville's already got more dogs and cats than people who want them," Willa protested.

It was true. Puppies and kittens were regularly deposited at the large collection of Dumpsters near the interstate to fend for themselves, or dropped from the bridge into the river to end things more quickly. This wasn't a town that was sentimental about such things.

"Those are all mutts," the HushMart minion said dismissively. "We'll sell purebreds here."

Willa absorbed this as she glanced around at the floor-to-ceiling shelves that seemed to stretch for miles.

"Can you point me toward the silver polish?" she asked. "I get so turned around in here."

"Straight that way, past the photo zone, third left into Household Care," the employee replied obligingly, before turning to thrust the chew toys in front of another shopper.

Willa made her ambling way through the photo zone, marveling at the variety of cameras and camera accessories she passed. Her husband Henry had been a photography aficionado, and Jiminy clearly enjoyed her Polaroids, but Willa herself had never had much interest. She appeared in photos if another pointed a camera at her, but she'd never played an active role in capturing images. When it came down to it, she was a fundamentally passive person—someone whom things happened to, rather than someone who made things happen. Though she and her granddaughter had never been close, until recently, she'd felt they shared this characteristic. But lately, Jiminy had seemed almost intent on shaking things up. It went beyond the Polaroids—there was a new restless questing to her that surprised and unsettled Willa. Willa didn't feel up to any fresh challenges. She felt weary and nervous.

"Now, what was it I was looking for?" she said aloud as she turned away from an aisle filled with albums.

What she wouldn't give to have someone sure and trustworthy beside her, whispering the answer in her ear.

———————

Don't be a coward, don't be a coward, Jiminy repeated in her head, waiting for it to seep in and give her strength. She'd climbed over the fence and taken a long walk down the hill toward the river, in search of fresh views and solitude to think and plan. But now she was trapped and terrified, looking around for weapons.

The rock in her hand wasn't large enough, and the only other things she could spot around her were twigs. Why didn't her grandmother have a dog? Some vicious, snarling, loyal dog who'd never let her go on walks by herself? If she got out of this alive, she swore she was going to get one.

"GO AWAY! GO! LEAVE ME ALONE!" she shouted at the top of her lungs.

They moved closer, and she backed away farther, trembling.

———————

"I guess she's really scared of them." Willa sighed as she stared out the dining room window. "That must've been why she was asking me how often they maul people. I thought she was joking. Who's scared of cows?"

Beside Willa, Lyn chuckled harder.

Willa was aware that this was the first time Lyn had smiled in her presence since their uncomfortable phone call. Even the yellowcake had only elicited an expressionless "Thanks." Willa beamed, grateful that her granddaughter's cowardice could bridge this divide.

"Should we draw straws to see who has to go rescue her?" she asked.

Lyn looked at her, eyes sparkling.

"She ain't my blood," Lyn replied. "So you can go draw your own straw."

Willa blinked in surprise, then burst out laughing, just as Lyn clutched her sleeve and pointed out the window.

"What's she doing? Did she just drop to the ground?"

They both stared in disbelief.

"Sweet Jesus, she's playing dead!" Lyn exclaimed.

Now they were both laughing uncontrollably, gasping for breath.

When Bo stuck his head into the room a moment later, Willa and Lyn were doubled over, holding onto each other, tears streaming from their eyes.

———————

Every time Jiminy screwed up enough courage to try to cross the field again, the cows would crowd around her, practically pressing into her flesh. There were bulls in there, too. Any one of them could charge her, trample her. The only ones that looked harmless were the calves, but they were the most dangerous of all, because they came with mothers who would kill to protect them. She knew she wasn't supposed to get between a calf and its mother, but when they all crowded around her like this, how could she keep track?

She never would have embarked on her walk in the first place if she'd thought there was any chance of this sort of encounter. Her grandmother had told her that the cattle had been moved to the fenced-in fields at the back of the farm for the next few months, so Jiminy had believed the fields between the house and the river were scary animal–free. But they'd appeared out of nowhere and descended upon her, and now she was pondering the very real possibility that her last moments alive would be filled with the smell of manure.

Just when Jiminy had closed her eyes to shut out the horror, she heard another voice.

"HUP, HUP, outta the way. HUP, HUP!"

She opened one eye tentatively. There was Bo, in the farm truck, parting the herd as he drove slowly toward her. He stopped a few feet away and climbed out. Unarmed, he continued his hup-hupping. The cattle didn't disperse, but they moved enough out of the way to allow him to reach her.

She flung her arms around his neck.

"Thank God you came," she exclaimed.

Only the fact that she was trembling stopped Bo from laughing.

"It's okay, I got you. We'll just walk back to the truck now."

"Watch out for the big one, I think he might charge," Jiminy whispered. "I'm just going to shut my eyes and hold onto your arm."

Bo nodded and guided her.

Even when Jiminy was safely in the passenger seat of the truck, she still worried they were in danger.

"Just hurry, but not too fast to agitate them," she said as the cattle continued to swarm. "If a couple of them charged, they could tip over the truck."

Bo continued to work hard not to laugh.

"They're not going to tip over the truck. They're not going to kill us. They don't want to kill us; they would like us to feed them. They're used to people walking or driving through the field to put more hay out for them to eat. That's why they hurry over to you. That's all they want—hay."

Jiminy absorbed this. Bo watched her cheeks blush crimson

as she looked anywhere but at him. He reached out to touch her arm.

"Hey," he said gently.

"I heard you the first time," she snapped. "Could you please just drive?"

Bo kept his hand on her arm.

"No."

Jiminy turned to him. On him, really.

"What kind of rescuer are you? Just get me out of here. Please! I'll drive, if that's the issue. Just scoot over."

She made a move to switch places with him.

"You're being silly," he said. "You've got nothing in the world to be scared of, do you understand?"

"Move!" she replied.

She tried clumsily to switch spots with him, throwing her leg over his lap and reaching her hand past him to grab the edge of the driver's seat to help hoist herself over. There wasn't anything graceful about her maneuver, and she was about to be stuck in an awkward position if he didn't help her out. So he obliged, scooting beneath her to the passenger side as Jiminy climbed all over him. It was the most intimate they'd ever been with each other, and for a brief moment all Bo could think about was how her breast had brushed his shoulder and how much her hair smelled like coconuts.

Jiminy was similarly flustered. She gripped the steering wheel to steady herself, acutely aware of how Bo's skin had felt against hers, and that she wanted to touch him more. Her cheeks blazing, she kept her eyes averted and hurried to switch the gears from park to drive. But she stopped abruptly, distress joining the other emotions playing across her features.

"What's the matter?" Bo asked.

Jiminy said something in a voice several decibels too soft for a human ear to decipher.

"What?" he asked again.

When she spoke this time, it was just barely audible.

"I didn't know this was stick. I don't know how to drive stick," she whispered.

When she looked up, Bo kissed her.

Jean Butrell was aiming her rifle at some deer when she heard tires on the gravel. She sighed and put the rifle down. At least the sound of the car would scare the deer away from her flowers for an hour or so. But if they came back when she was alone, she'd pop 'em. To think that she'd once put a salt lick out there for their enjoyment. How naïve she'd been. Salt one day, prize-winning geraniums the next. They deserved to die.

The car had to be Jiminy, who'd been coming to Jean's regularly ever since she'd discovered that Jean had an Internet connection, a rare and precious hookup among Willa's friends. Most of them didn't consider themselves members of the technological age and were happy to be bypassed by tweets and blogs, even by online shopping, which many of them would have found extremely convenient. The Home Shopping Network and the telephone were still their tools of choice.

Jean was an aberration. She'd had an Internet connection for five years now, and prized it above all else. During thunderstorms, she dreaded losing electricity almost solely because it would mean getting knocked offline. She had a real passion for games like Halo 3 and the ones on Pogo—the kind you could log on to and play against people from all over the world. Her grandsons had introduced her to them over a Christmas holiday, and she'd come straight home and ordered up service. She was addicted.

"Knock, knock," Jiminy called from the porch.

"Who's there?" Jean called.

She hoped for a knock-knock joke, but Willa's granddaughter was too literal.

"It's Jiminy."

"Come on in," Jean replied, covering her sigh with a bright smile. "Can I pour you some iced tea? It's hot out there."

Jiminy shook her head.

"No, thank you, I don't need anything. How's it going?"

Jean appreciated the attempt at small talk.

"Oh, I'm all right. My suck-egg dog of a son called again, but I screened him."

The elder son who'd confiscated her driver's license. Not the one who'd fathered the two grandsons who'd taught her how to play blackjack online. That son was a saint.

"Maybe he's just worried about you," Jiminy offered.

"I hope so! I hope he worries his little conniving, controlling squirrel brain sick," Jean replied. "The computer's all yours, sweetheart. I don't have a game appointment for another few hours."

"Thanks," Jiminy said gratefully.

She hurried to the living room desk and logged herself on to her saved searches. There was the article that she'd come across the previous afternoon and been yearning to investigate further. Jiminy scanned it quickly, looking for the name she'd spotted.

Were it not for the tireless efforts of Carlos Castaverde, this long-ago murder would have remained unsolved, languishing

*in the cold case file cabinet in the basement of the Putner
County Courthouse. But Mr. Castaverde refused to let justice
die along with an innocent victim.*

That was it: Carlos Castaverde. According to this article and
another one in the *Greenham Gazette*, Carlos Castaverde was a
persistent journalist-lawyer who had successfully reopened
and solved seven civil rights cold cases. His latest efforts had
led to the conviction and imprisonment of an eighty-four-year-
old ex-Klansman who had kidnapped and lynched a young
man by the name of Jackson Honder for "leering" at a white
woman in September 1955. According to law enforcement officials at the time, no one in Jackson Honder's small town had
seen or heard anything, and no arrests were ever made. Until
over a half century later, when Carlos Castaverde began investigating. After interviewing Honder's brother and sisters, along
with some neighbors and a sheriff's deputy, Castaverde determined that contrary to the official record, pretty much everyone in town knew exactly who had committed the murder. A
few more months of legwork and two eyewitness accounts
later, and Carlos had his man. The Honder family expressed
their incredulity and gratitude to the *Greenham Gazette:*

> *"When Carlos first came round, I thought, let's let bygones
> be bygones and be done with it," said Honder's sister Mag-
> gie Jayce, aged eighty-two. "But now that Jackson's killer is
> behind bars, I feel like somethin' that was turned upside down
> in the world just got set right again."*

The killer was someone who'd continued to live right alongside the Honder family for fifty-three years. And they'd all

known. All of them. Jiminy couldn't imagine how that must have felt. How do you greet a man who murdered your brother? How do you stand in line at the post office with him, or pass him in the dairy aisle, or pump gas alongside him, knowing all the while? How did they stand it? And would they just have kept on standing it, day after day, had Carlos not come along?

She Googled Carlos Castaverde and immediately came across several hate websites. One claimed he was an illegal immigrant with a grudge against red-blooded Americans. Another listed his home address and offered a bounty for his head.

A more friendly site called him an unsung hero and thanked him for his service. Carlos himself didn't have a website and seemed to prefer a low profile, though Jiminy was able to find a bio piece on him in the *Greenham Gazette* that detailed how, after being raised in Texarkana by a Caucasian mother and Mexican father, Carlos had gotten his degree in journalism and then put himself through law school at night while working for a string of small town newspapers. He'd first made a name for himself seven years ago, when, in the course of covering a disputed school board election, he'd stumbled across an account of an unsolved shooting that had taken place in 1964. His subsequent investigation had eventually led to the conviction and incarceration of the superintendent of schools. The town had been outraged; the victim's family, grateful.

Since then, Carlos Castaverde had opened and pursued six other cases. He hadn't won convictions in all of them, but he had forced several towns to confront their unpleasant pasts. Not all of them appreciated the experience, and they'd made their wrath known. In a short interview conducted after the Jackson Honder case was won, the forty-four-year-old Castaverde was asked what made him get up every day and pursue the life he'd chosen. He'd answered, "Consideration of the alternative."

Abrupt gunshots startled Jiminy out of her admiring reverie. She whirled around, her heart throbbing furiously.

"Dammit, missed again," Jean muttered as she sauntered in from the backyard, a rifle slung over one shoulder. "Sorry for the noise, I was trying to shoot the geranium-gobblin' demon deer," she explained.

Jiminy breathed in deeply, trying to calm herself down. It was only Jean. And everything was still alive.

"Do you hunt often?" she managed to ask.

Jiminy herself had never held a gun.

"Oh, darlin', that's not huntin', that's gardenin'," Jean answered.

Jiminy nodded, eyeing the rifle.

"Where do you keep that?"

Jean glanced down at the gun.

"Wherever. In the corner by my bed, in the car occasionally— back when I was allowed to drive—but it's by the kitchen sink generally. So I can grab it quick when those overgrown rats with antlers come around."

Jean finally registered the terror in Jiminy's eyes and left the room to put the gun away somewhere out of sight. When she returned, she was carrying two glasses of iced tea.

"I know you said you didn't want any, but house rules are you gotta have at least a glass in exchange for computer privileges."

Jiminy smiled and took the glass Jean offered.

"I should be bringing *you* things," Jiminy said. "I really appreciate you letting me come here. I'm happy to get the chance to work on this stuff."

Jean nodded indulgently.

"And what is it exactly that you're working on?" she asked.

Willa had told her a little bit, but not much. Jean had initially appreciated being spared the details, but now her curiosity was getting the better of her.

"I want to find out more about who killed Lyn's husband and daughter," Jiminy said. "I can't believe their murders were never solved. You knew them, didn't you?"

"Of course," Jean answered.

Fayeville was a small place, and it had only been smaller back then. She'd known Edward since they were kids, and Lyn since he'd married her. The same year Jean had married her husband, Floyd the prankster.

Jean suddenly didn't feel like talking anymore, but Jiminy was looking at her expectantly.

"Do you have any idea who might have killed them?" Jiminy asked.

Jean stared out the window, toward the woods that bordered her lawn. She stared a little too long.

"You do, don't you?" Jiminy pressed. "You know something."

Jean closed her eyes, wishing she'd been raised to know how to politely kick a guest out of her house. She felt a migraine coming on.

———

The river that curved around Fayeville was slow and cold. It was filled with rainbow trout and water moccasins that slithered across the surface and made their home along the bank. Jiminy had never been on or in the river. She'd never fished it, never swam it, never even stuck a hand or toe in it. Now that she knew about Edward and the first Jiminy, it made sense to her that the people who would've naturally taken her to do such things avoided the river as a matter of course. Still, you'd think they would've provided her with some substitute. You'd think they might have brought her to the pool in town, particularly on the hot summer days that made kids fall into sweaty boredom comas. But Jiminy had never been there, either. Until now.

As she pulled into the parking lot, she wished she wasn't alone. At least there weren't any cattle in sight.

The Fayeville Municipal Pool was shaped like a kidney bean and included a waterslide that was slightly the worse for wear, though the kids flinging themselves down it didn't seem to mind. On the far side of the pool stood a tall lifeguard chair positioned to watch over all. The lifeguard was the one Jiminy had come to see.

Before she could make her way to him, someone called her name.

"Jiminy Davis, is that you?"

An enormously pregnant belly sandwiched by a bikini had asked the question. Technically, the mouth on the head attached to the belly had asked it, but all Jiminy could focus on was the belly. She forced herself to look up from it to acknowledge its owner's face.

"Suze?" Jiminy asked.

Suze Connors had grown up on the farm across the river from Willa's.

The smiling round face nodded.

"Yep, it's me. Can you believe it?"

Jiminy wasn't sure she'd ever seen a more pregnant woman.

"Congratulations!" Jiminy cried. "You look great!"

"Thank you, what a nice thing to hear," Suze responded. "Some people say I shouldn't be wearing a two-piece, but I say they should GET THEIR OWN LIFE," she continued in a near shout, directing the accusatory part of her sentence toward a slender woman suntanning a few chairs over. The woman rolled her eyes and whispered something to her friend. Both of them giggled. Suze fumed.

"So, when are you due?" Jiminy asked, attempting to avert a rumble.

She was taken aback by Suze's sudden fury. Jiminy remembered her being a mild-mannered girl—someone she'd played with a handful of times during her childhood visits.

"Tomorrow," Suze answered. "But my first three were all a week late, so I'm not holding my breath."

"This is your *fourth* kid?" Jiminy asked.

Suze was nodding.

"Bryce! Savanna! Come meet Jiminy," she called to a blond-haired boy and girl who'd been playing on the waterslide. "Melody's with her grandma," she explained to Jiminy as her kids started swimming for the pool ladder.

"Oh, don't bother them, it's okay . . . ," Jiminy attempted.

But the kids were already hurrying to obey their mom. Jiminy was surprised at how quickly they were in front of her, gazing upward.

"Jiminy and I used to play when we were around your age," Suze told her son. "Are you here for a while?" she asked Jiminy.

Jiminy wasn't sure how to answer.

"I think so. Probably another few weeks, at least."

"We gotta get together then!" Suze cried.

Jiminy nodded.

"Sure, that'd be great, definitely. I mean, you'll probably be pretty busy with your baby and your other kids, but if you get some free time . . . Are you married?"

Suze looked offended.

"Well, I should hope so! What kind of girl do you think I am?"

"I'm sorry, I didn't mean to—I just didn't want to assume—of course you're married."

"Brad's on a tour of duty overseas now, but he should be home by Christmas. SAVANNAH, DON'T YOU DARE PUT THAT IN YOUR MOUTH!"

Jiminy jumped. Behind her, Savannah released a small frog she'd caught in the grass by the side of the pool. She obeyed her mother, but she wasn't happy about it.

The shouting had caught the lifeguard's attention. He stood up quickly, gave a disapproving glance, then resumed his vigil. For an old man, he seemed remarkably spry and alert.

"I need to go," Jiminy said to Suze. "It's good to see you again, and meet your kids. I'll see you around."

Suze smiled and nodded, but she was already preoccupied with helping her son wrestle a pair of flippers onto his feet.

"Don't forget to come see me," she replied distractedly.

Jiminy weaved past Savannah and made her way to the lifeguard chair, aware of how pale her skin was compared to the tanned bodies around her. Looking down at her arms and legs, she saw that her skin was even whiter than usual, thanks to the SPF50 she'd failed to completely rub in.

The lifeguard stared down at her. He was the ruler of this domain and prided himself on knowing everyone. This small, pale woman standing below him was a stranger, though she resembled people he knew. She'd have to explain herself.

"May I help you?" he asked.

"Are you Walton Trawler?" Jiminy asked.

"Indeed, I am," he answered.

Walton was old, certainly, but he emanated a youthfulness that matched the energy of the kids surrounding him. He'd been the town doctor for fifty years and now filled his retirement with volunteer work and various other projects. His face was tanned and wrinkled, and he wore a weathered fishing hat to protect his bald head. His swimming trunks were decorated with fuschia palm trees.

"Who are you?" he inquired.

He wasn't as friendly as Jiminy had hoped he'd be.

"I'm Jiminy Davis, Willa Hunt's granddaughter. I'm interested in learning more about Fayeville, and Jean Butrell suggested I talk to you. She said you're kind of the town historian, published and all."

Walton had written several books about the region. He looked more intently at Jiminy, before shifting his gaze to scan the pool.

"I can't talk now, I'm on the job. Stop by Grady's Grill this evening and we'll chat."

Jiminy nodded. It didn't seem as though he was going to say anything more to her, so she turned to walk away.

"You have your grandpa's eyes, you know," Walton said.

Jiminy paused and turned back.

"Really?"

No one had ever told her this before.

"Spittin' image," Walton nodded. "You must break your grandma's heart."

———

Roy Tomlins always took his lunch break on the benches of the courtyard lawn, and he generally stopped by Grady's Grill for his post-work beer. He liked the feel of Grady's—the sawdust on the floor, the ashtrays on every table, the counter lined with bottles of local hot sauce. He liked that it was generally filled with men he knew, with men he'd known all his life.

They were dying off now, the men of his generation. There were only a handful of them left, and they were vastly outnumbered by the women. Old women live forever, Roy mused. His wife would likely outlast him by decades, continuing to be a waste of space long after he was gone. Roy hated feeling overwhelmed by women, hated the way they banded together when their husbands died off. There was no helping the situation though. This was what it had come to. At least now that Roy had grasped the reality that the guys were on their way out, he felt a new appreciation for their company.

"Evenin', Grady."

"Evenin', Roy. People still sending letters?"

Grady liked to tease that the postal service was on its last legs now that so many people had electronic ways to communicate. Grady himself didn't email anyone. He still sent letters and occasional care packages to his son and daughter on the West Coast, which Roy knew because Roy monitored everything that crossed his counter.

Of course Roy was well aware that opening someone else's mail was a serious criminal offense, so he only did it when he was really curious. He kept a steamer in the closet of his office to make it easy, and then he'd seal the envelopes back up good as new. Working in the postal office was an excellent way to keep tabs on the town, a role that Roy took extremely seriously. He considered himself a patriot, first and foremost, and was therefore positive that his watchdog actions were justified, even necessary.

The bell over the door announced a new arrival as Roy was

trying to make out the label on a hot sauce bottle in the shape of a naked woman. He turned slightly and looked over his shoulder. It was Walton, which he should've expected.

"Evenin', Walton. Save any lives today?" Grady asked.

"Not yet," Walton answered.

Walton took his regular seat at the table by the window and began rolling one of his cigarettes. He took pride in only smoking homegrown tobacco. And he restricted himself to smoking only one cigarette a day, mainly because he'd been a doctor for so long and felt he had to keep up appearances. He ate an apple a day also, and hoped that the two canceled each other out.

"Howdy, Walton," Roy grunted.

"Evenin', Roy."

Noticing how hard Roy was studying the Some Like It Hot Sauce, Grady grabbed it and handed it over.

"Well, I'll be," Roy exclaimed, running his fingers over the plastic breasts. "This really local?"

"Yep," Grady affirmed. "Some guy over in Baileyville makes it. I can get you your own if you're interested. She don't come life-size, though," he added with a chuckle.

"How does she taste?" Roy asked with a grin. "Dish me some of that barbequed brisket so I can test 'er."

From behind the counter, Grady complied. Roy splashed a generous dose on the brisket and took a bite, then grimaced. Grady nodded knowingly as he put the bottle back on the shelf.

"I know," Grady lamented. "Great package. Godawful flavor."

"You coulda saved me the trouble," Roy grumbled.

Grady shrugged.

"Everyone's got their own tastes," he replied. "You mighta liked it."

Roy looked glumly at his remaining barbequed brisket.

"At least give me something good to forget that," he requested.

Grady rummaged beneath the counter.

"Here's the best we've got. Also new, not as sexy."

Grady squirted some hot sauce out of a plain plastic bottle. Roy sniffed it warily, then took a bite. He smiled, brisket sticking out between his teeth.

"Now, that's a hot sauce," he pronounced happily. "What's that one? I'll take some of it to make Helen's pork chops edible."

Grady turned the bottle to show him.

"In Foo-ego?" Roy asked.

"En Fuego," Walton said from over Roy's shoulder. "It means 'on fire' in Spanish."

Roy was startled by Walton's sudden closeness. He jerked a little, then pushed his plate away.

"No, thanks. I don't eat Mexican."

Grady shrugged.

"Juan from Tortillas gave it to me. It's good stuff," Grady said.

Grady said "tortillas" like it rhymed with "vanilla" or "Godzilla."

"Tor-tee-yas," Walton corrected. "The two 'l's make a 'y' sound, and the 'i' is pronounced like a long 'e.'"

Both Grady and Roy ignored him. Walton tended to know too much about everything.

Tortillas had opened three months ago, much to the surprise of the Fayeville residents. Some of them were aware that the apartments at the western end of town had seen an influx of Mexicans in recent years, but no one had really tuned in to just how many were now actually calling Fayeville home. Previously, the immigrants' presence had been temporary. A group of them would arrive to help work the harvest and then leave again. Then, suddenly, they'd stopped leaving. And then more of them had come. There were plenty of jobs for them, that wasn't the problem. It was just a surprising development for a town that had thought of itself as strictly black and white—and mostly white at that—for its entire history. Missis sippi wasn't Texas; this was the Deep South. And this was brand-new.

"I thought you only bought local stuff," Walton said.

"It is local," Grady answered. "I told you, Juan gave it to me. He makes it."

Roy just shook his head.

The bell over the door announced another patron.

Roy shifted in his seat, hoping to see their old friend Travis Brayer walking in. He knew that Travis was still bedridden— had been bedridden since the month his son announced his race for governor—but Roy hoped nonetheless. He loved Travis, and he planned to visit him soon. They had business to discuss.

It was a young woman. As the door slapped shut behind her, she looked around nervously, like a trapped rabbit. She struck Roy as vaguely familiar, but he couldn't place her. He turned back to his beer.

Jiminy had never been inside Grady's Grill before. Her eyes watering from the thick cloud of cigarette smoke, she walked over to the table Walton had returned to.

"Is now an okay time?" she asked.

Walton glanced at Roy and Grady, then indicated the empty chair across from him.

"So you're interested in Fayeville history."

Jiminy nodded as she settled in opposite him.

"Actually, in a very specific time period," she answered.

"The late sixties. And 1966 in particular. Do you remember that year?"

Walton took a long drag on his cigarette. He nodded slowly, watching Jiminy with an inscrutable expression.

"That was way before you were born," he said.

"But there was another Jiminy alive then. Jiminy Waters. Did you happen to know her? She was young, only seventeen in 1966. And her father Edward. Did you know them?"

Walton tapped his cigarette against the ashtray. Across the room, Roy shifted his weight on his stool.

"I knew 'em. Edward was a carpenter. Could carve anything outta wood. Anything t'all."

Jiminy paused. She hadn't heard this before, hadn't even thought to ask anyone what Edward had done for a living. She'd thought of him as Lyn's husband and Jiminy's father and a murdered man. Just being these things had seemed occupation enough.

"Did he work with my grandpa then?" Jiminy asked.

To help pay for their small farm, Henry Hunt had done carpentry jobs all over Fayeville, according to Willa.

Walton nodded.

"Edward did the woodwork and Henry handled the business side, since he was obviously who folks wanted to deal with."

This was also news to Jiminy, who had always pictured her grandfather as a master craftsman. She'd imagined that same talent flowed through her veins, hence her fascination with hardware store catalogues and penchant for buying build-it-yourself furniture.

The revelation that Henry hadn't actually possessed that talent came as a bit of a shock. She thought of a doll she'd once found in her grandpa's workshop closet—an exquisitely carved wooden boy. She'd gone on imaginary safaris with him, engineered elaborate pillow forts with him, told him her deepest, most precious secrets. She'd imagined her grandpa carving him carefully, lovingly for her, before he even knew she was going to exist. That wooden boy had convinced her she belonged in her family. Had he actually been Edward's handiwork all along?

"So were my grandpa and Edward friends?" Jiminy asked.

Walton took another long drag on his cigarette, then exhaled slowly. Jiminy coughed into her hand and turned toward the window.

"They were close," Walton answered. "Henry was the boss, but they were close. Edward and Lyn lived just down the hill at that time, in a house by the river that your grandpa owned. So they were tenants as well."

Jiminy nodded.

"And Lyn worked with my grandmother," she said.

"For your grandmother, yes, though Lyn worked the farm alongside Henry and Edward for years before Willa came along. And then Lyn worked for the Brayers for a time, too."

Jiminy looked up quickly.

"For the Brayers? Really?" she asked.

Grady started coughing from across the room, and Jiminy could see out of the corner of her eye that he wasn't covering his mouth.

"Uh-huh," Walton answered.

Jiminy contemplated this for a moment.

"Was Lyn close with the Brayers?" she asked.

Walton took another drag on his cigarette.

"I wouldn't say that."

Jiminy stared at him expectantly, waiting for more information, but none came.

"Did anyone have a problem with them?" she asked finally.

"With who?"

"With Lyn and Edward and my grandparents. With the way they did things, the way they were. With their closeness."

Walton regarded her, as sizzling noises escaped from the kitchen.

"Pretty much everyone," he answered.

Jiminy held his gaze, determined not to blink. She had more questions, but she suddenly felt claustrophobic in this hot, smoky, germy place. She stood abruptly.

"I gotta go," she said. "Thanks for your time."

She needed to get away. She needed to breathe uncontaminated air. She'd tackle this again, but right now she needed to flee. She felt old men eyes on her as she hurried toward the door.

"Be sure to come back, ya hear?" jangled in her ears along with the screen door bells. She thought she heard chuckling, too, but she couldn't be sure.

JIMINY RECOGNIZED BO'S DEEP LAUGH along with the distinctive voice of Bea Arthur coming from the trailer. The TV volume was too high for anyone to hear her knocks, so she stuck her head in gingerly, trying not to startle anyone. She didn't succeed. Bo jumped up from where he'd been sprawled on the couch, and abruptly turned off the TV with an embarrassed look on his face. If Jiminy hadn't already heard some of the dialogue, she would have assumed from his reaction that he'd been watching porn.

"Is that *The Golden Girls*?" she inquired.

"What, that?" Bo asked, pointing to the TV as though he were an alien who'd just been dropped off and couldn't be sure of what things were called on this planet. "Nuh-uh, no. Or, maybe. I wasn't paying too much attention to what I flipped past between games."

"Dude, what happened to Dorothy?" a voice called from the back of the trailer.

Jiminy turned to see a stocky redhead emerge from the bathroom, brushing his teeth.

"Oh," he said, as he spotted Jiminy.

"Jiminy, this is Cole," Bo said. "Cole, Jiminy."

Bo had told Jiminy about Cole—his best friend from growing up, his roommate for the summer—but she hadn't actually encountered him until now.

"Hey," Jiminy said.

Cole stared back.

"We were just watching a game," he claimed.

"I heard," Jiminy replied. "It's too bad, because I love *The Golden Girls.*"

Both men looked relieved.

"Oh, yeah?" Bo asked.

Jiminy nodded.

"They're the best, right?" Cole enthused. "Turn it back on, Bo."

The TV sprang to life as Bo happily complied.

"I'll go back so you can see it from the beginning," he offered.

"You have it recorded?" Jiminy asked.

"All of 'em," Bo confirmed.

He was looking sheepish again. And handsome, in his white T-shirt and jeans. After Cole disappeared back into the bathroom, Jiminy leaned in and kissed him.

"How'd the studying go?"

"Good," Bo replied, sliding his arm around her and pulling her into him. "Ask me anything about the regulation of kidney function, or just kidneys in general. Anything. I own the kidneys now."

"Why do so many people shape swimming pools like them?"

Bo paused. He nodded his head sagely, as though he was admiring the sophistication of the question.

"Just know that I know and that the answer is classified. Top secret renal reasons, is all I can say."

"Hmm. I assumed it had something to do with how often kids pee in them."

"I see you have high-level clearance," Bo replied in an exaggeratedly impressed tone.

Jiminy laughed. She looked around the small trailer. It belonged to Cole's family, who owned the cattle farm on which it was parked. Cole's parents resided in the large house a half mile away, but Cole preferred the trailer in the summertime. He worked the farm during the day and applied to sports agencies in his free time. He'd only received rejections so far, but he firmly believed he was the next undiscovered Jerry Maguire. He knew it would take a little time to make his mark. He wasn't in a big hurry.

"All right, I'm outta here, see ya," Cole called as he exited the trailer. "Nice to meet you, Jiminy, don't be a stranger."

Jiminy wondered if Cole really had someplace to go, or if he was just clearing out for her and Bo's sake.

As the sound of Cole's footfalls receded, Bo pulled Jiminy onto his lap.

"How was the pool?" he asked as he twisted a piece of her hair around his finger. "Besides being shaped like a human organ."

Jiminy shrugged.

"Okay, I guess. You know what it's like."

But Bo was shaking his head.

"Nope. Never been there."

Jiminy didn't believe him.

"Seriously," he insisted.

"You're kidding me. Not even once?"

"I've driven by. But I've never actually gone in."

"Why not?" Jiminy asked. "The slide looks fun if you're ten years old with a death wish. You were ten once. Didn't you want to go?"

Bo thought about it. He could remember being ten years old. Could remember how hot the sun felt on his head and shoulders in July in the yard where he'd set up his toy soldiers in the dirt. He'd never gone to the pool, but he'd gone to the river once. He'd been scared of it, but he'd overcome his hesitation and jumped off a big rock into the surprisingly frigid water. He remembered how his lungs had frozen up, how his blood had suddenly felt like ice water in his veins. And how a cloud had blocked the sun just when he'd climbed out on the bank, causing him to shiver on a hot July day.

Jiminy suddenly clapped her hand over her mouth.

"Oh my God, were you not allowed in the pool?" she asked. "Because people . . . because of . . ."

Bo snapped back to the present, away from his river memory.

"It wasn't anything official," he answered. "I didn't care much about going anyway, but I doubt it's changed. Did you see any black kids there?"

Jiminy shook her head. Why hadn't she noticed that earlier?

"Well, when I was driving home today, I saw some Mexican kids on a Slip 'n Slide," Bo said. "So we slum it a little, but there are ways around the system."

Loud, canned laughter sounded from the television, but both of them had lost track of the story line. Bo wanted Jiminy to take her pitying eyes someplace else. He didn't want that emotion introduced into their relationship.

"You know what? I should probably get some more studying done," he said suddenly, shifting her off his lap and standing up.

"Really?" Jiminy asked. "I thought we were doing something."

"Maybe later. Let's talk later."

Jiminy nodded slowly, clearly confused. She stood and began to leave the trailer, then paused and turned back.

"Did you know your aunt Lyn worked for the Brayers at one point?" she asked.

Bo stared at her a moment.

"No, I didn't. She can't stand the Brayers."

"Really?" Jiminy asked. "Why not?"

"She never said," Bo answered. "It's just something I always knew. We used to take the long way home from school just to avoid going by their place."

Jiminy nodded thoughtfully, her face full of further questions. Bo studied her and internally debated whether he could reverse course and invite her to stay. But now she was walking away, across the grass, toward Willa's Buick. She started to turn back again, but stopped herself and climbed into the car. Above her, the sky was bruised with another dying day.

B Y THE TIME Juan Gonzales bought the building that would become Tortillas, it had stood empty for nearly thirty years. In its basement, he found furniture that he assumed was from the abandoned movie theater next door: an old ticket-taking booth, a broken counter, and five wooden chairs. The chairs didn't look like actual theater chairs to Juan, but he hadn't examined them too closely. When his wife saw them, she decided they'd look nice arranged on the front patio of the restaurant, and she commissioned him to clean them up. Juan personally didn't consider it worth the effort, but he enjoyed the perks that came with keeping Rosa happy, so he had bent to his task with a rag and bucket of soapy water.

Once the layers of dust and dirt had been cleaned away, the chairs actually did look pretty good. They were made of wood and impressively crafted. They were also each adorned with a shiny metal plate, previously unnoticeable thanks to the grime, attached to the top of the seat back. Engraved on each plate were the initials "K.S.O." Juan assumed they were the initials of the company that had owned the theater, or made the chairs, or distributed the films. He had pointed them out to Rosa and rubbed them harder to make them shine. She'd smiled excitedly before returning inside to check on the specially made tortillas for which their new restaurant was named.

"Where'd you get those?"

Juan was pleasantly surprised to see Grady standing just at the edge of the patio. Juan admired the success of Grady's Grill and hoped his own restaurant could inspire such a loyal clientele.

"They came with the place," Juan answered. "In the basement."

Juan recognized the empty bottle Grady carried in his hand and wondered if he was going to be asked for his hot sauce recipe. He'd sell Grady all the sauce he wanted, but he wasn't going to reveal its secret, and he hoped that wouldn't make things awkward.

"They don't belong to you, I don't think," Grady said.

Juan waited for him to say more. Grady became self-conscious.

"I mean, I s'pose if they came with your place, then you'd think they're yours, a'course. But those belonged to the Brayer family. I recognize them."

Juan looked down at the chairs he'd just spent an hour and a half cleaning. Rosa had really had a vision of how these chairs were going to look outside of Tortillas. She wanted them arranged just so; he knew the way her mind worked. The same mind that had decided their daughter would be named "Penelope" and nicknamed "Pen" long before they'd even conceived. The mind that planned the menu months in advance, that obsessed over colors in flower displays, that wouldn't let anyone help her make her signature empanadas. Juan didn't want to have to tell Rosa that her chair brainstorm wasn't going to happen.

"I think the Brayers just lost track of 'em," Grady was saying. "But those gold plates are pretty recognizable."

Surely they weren't real gold. Was that why this was such an issue? Juan wondered. Now Rosa would be even more upset if he let them go.

"What does 'K.S.O.' stand for?" Juan asked.

Grady straightened.

"Something someone else knows about, I guess," he replied. "I'll tell Travis Brayer you've got his chairs. Maybe he'll be fine with you keepin' 'em, you never know."

Juan nodded slowly. From the tone of Grady's voice he could tell that Grady believed that Travis would not be fine with Juan keeping them.

"It's just that, in this country, you can't come in and take things that rightfully belong to others, that's all," Grady said.

Juan remained silent. Grady reddened a bit.

"Anyway, I love that sauce a yours," he continued. "Could I get some more? I'll pay for it, a'course."

Juan looked Grady directly in the eyes.

"I'm all out," he lied.

Grady held Juan's gaze for a moment, then looked off at the purple sky.

"Well, let me know when you make more and have some to spare. I really do like it."

Juan nodded.

"Sure, amigo. I'll let you know."

Walton hadn't told Jiminy that he'd been in the room when Lyn had come to see the bodies of her husband and daughter on that June night in 1966. He hadn't told Jiminy much of anything, really. With Roy and Grady listening, he'd said a tiny bit about Edward, Lyn, Willa, and Henry, but there was so much more. Way too much more.

When Henry Hunt had found the bodies of Edward and Jiminy Waters two weeks after they'd gone missing, he'd brought them by the hospital to get them cleaned up. After some strong resistance, Walton had tended to them. And then Lyn had arrived.

Walton closed his eyes at the memory. In fifty years as Fayeville's doctor, he'd seen a lot of pain. And in all of that time, nothing matched the crumpling of Lyn Waters.

She didn't make a scene, like some people did when confronted with the corpses of loved ones. She didn't pound her fists into the wall, she didn't tear at her hair or explode into paroxysms of sobs. She looked at them—one long look at her dead husband's face, one long look at her dead daughter's. Then she stared straight ahead, into a void visible only to her, and her face fell off of itself. Walton didn't know how else to describe it: As far as he could tell, whatever was alive in Lyn had poured out of her in that moment. It had streamed out of her nostrils, and her slightly parted lips, and the corners of her eyes. In a rush, it had fled.

Walton had gone cold at the sight. Henry had hurried to take Lyn in his arms, but she'd held up her hand, stopping him with a silent command. She'd looked at them both with hollow eyes, then turned and walked out of the room. From then on, Lyn had seemed no more than a shell of a human, filled only with haunted echoes of previous life.

Walton hadn't mentioned any of this to Willa's granddaughter, but that June night was seared into his memory. After Lyn left, one of Edward's brothers had come to collect the bodies. There'd been a funeral that Walton hadn't attended, but he knew where the gravesite was, and over the years, he'd found himself occasionally driving past it at night after leaving the hospital. On this night, he found himself headed there again.

He steered his car off the pavement and continued up the

dirt road. At the top of the ridge, he stopped to take in the view. The lights of HushMart flickered behind him, but before him the hills rolled out as far as a person could see. By the soft glow of the nearly full moon, he could make out the inky curves of the Allehany River as it flowed around and between and against, patiently wearing down the land.

Walton climbed out of his car and walked up the slope to the huge magnolia tree, aware that the ache in his knee was worsening. He'd managed to hang onto all his original joints thus far, but he saw artificial ones in his future. He was under no illusions about being in decline.

At the start of his retirement, Walton had written several books about the history and geology of Fayeville. In one chapter about Fayeville plants, he'd actually featured the tree that was now before him. It was enormous, and the smell of its flowers could be sweetly overpowering, especially when a breeze blew down from the bluff. Amid the fallen blossoms on the ground were headstones, marking the graves of dozens buried in the magnolia's shadow. Nobody white was buried here—there was a county-maintained cemetery in town for them. This magnolia tree cemetery was more haphazard and bureaucracy-free, maintained by people nobody paid. It was where the black residents of Fayeville had been burying their dead for over two hundred years.

Walton fished a pocket flashlight out and shined it on the spot he remembered. There they were—two rough-edged stone slabs that peeked six inches above the ground. They'd risen higher forty years ago, but the gravestones were settled in and tilting now. They seemed at peace.

As a rule, Walton didn't believe in visiting people's graves. He never checked in on the final resting plots of his own friends and relatives—he preferred to remember how they'd been alive. And he considered himself extremely rational. He knew the ground only held decomposing bio-matter, not the spirits or souls of the departed. But ever since he'd watched Lyn fly out of herself and walk away, he'd felt drawn to the place where her loved ones had been laid to rest. In visiting their graves, he attempted to pay them some kind of tribute, or apology.

It wasn't until he had turned to walk back to his car that his eye caught the glint of white on the wooden cross that marked the start of the cemetery. He trained his flashlight on it and stepped closer, wincing at the pinch in his knee. The letters were big, and freshly painted, he guessed. The empty spray-paint can from HushMart was discarded nearby.

Walton exhaled slowly. There'd been a time when those letters had seemed omnipresent around Fayeville. There'd been a time when Walton had identified with them. He'd learned since then, and now the sight of the recently branded "K.S.O." on the cross made him weary. And worried.

"Was I wrong to chase her off?" Bo asked.

He was tossing a football with Cole, syncing his regret to the spiraling ball. He imagined hurling his doubts away from him with each arm pump. Unfortunately, they kept slamming back into him.

"Dude, you don't want her pity," Cole replied with a shrug.

Cole had been Bo's best friend since they'd met in Little League as five-year-olds. Whereas Bo had always been talkative and bright, Cole was a man of few words, many of which were "dude." Still, the two of them understood each other perfectly.

"Yeah, I don't need this, you know?" Bo said. "I should just stick to my plan—lay low, save money, get ready for med school, get out of here."

Bo waited for Cole to agree with him.

"But she is something," Bo sighed.

Jiminy had been an unexpected distraction. Her hesitancy intrigued him. Her flashes of assertiveness unnerved him. And kissing her had been a revelation. Bo wanted to kiss her again, and the thought that he might not be able to made him frantic.

"Damn," he said quietly to himself.

He knew that in this town there were plenty of reasons to think twice about pursuing her. Of all people, Cole knew this, too. Cole had fought many fights over his friendship with Bo.

"Dude," Cole said, as he caught and held the ball.

Bo stared at him, wondering if there would be more.

"Go get her."

Bo broke into a grin. They knew this place. They were of this place. But they were young.

———

Jiminy was reading outside, scratching a mosquito bite with one hand and swinging her free-hanging leg back and forth so that it made a pendulum shadow against the smooth stone patio. She looked up when Bo's truck pulled into the driveway, grateful that if a person kept her ears open, the gravel made it impossible for anyone to sneak up.

"Hey," she said, as she half-closed her book.

She started to smile but held herself back, letting only the edges of it creep into her voice. She wasn't sure whether she and Bo were liking each other or not. She'd been confused by their last encounter.

"What are your thoughts on Dairy Queen?" he asked.

She closed her book all the way.

———

"This is the only thing cows are good for," Jiminy said as she licked her chocolate-dipped vanilla cone. "And hamburgers. And cheese. In that order."

They were sitting at a picnic table in the grass between the road and the Dairy Queen parking lot.

"Have you always been scared of them?" Bo asked between bites of his caramel sundae.

Jiminy nodded.

"They're evil," she whispered.

"They're dumb," Bo offered.

"That's the worst kind of evil," Jiminy replied.

"That's debatable," Bo countered with a grin. "Evil geniuses are no picnic."

"Fair point," Jiminy conceded.

It was a hot day and their ice cream was melting fast. Jiminy's hand was already covered in sticky melted sugar.

"Hang on, I'm gonna grab some napkins," she said as she jumped up and crossed the parking lot.

She'd just made it inside the Dairy Queen doorway when she ran into Suze Connors, who was wearing a midriff halter top and looking even more pregnant than before—something Jiminy wouldn't have thought possible.

"Jiminy!" Suze yipped affectionately. "Ma, look who it is! I told you Jiminy was in town."

Suze's mother was a damp, solidly built woman who looked Jiminy up and down with a lazy flicker of her eyelids. These languid lids were the most active part of a round, clammy face. When she smiled, her teeth came out as slowly as a snail from its shell.

"Howya doin'?" she asked.

"I'm fine, thank you," Jiminy said. "You're about to get another grandbaby, I see."

She'd never used the word "grandbaby" in her life, but it seemed to fit with this place and these circumstances. Mrs. Connors nodded.

"Any minute now," she said. "And then it'll just take another minute for Suze to get pregnant again."

"Oh, Mama, it will not," Suze replied, rolling her eyes at Jiminy.

Jiminy smiled sympathetically, unsure of whether she meant it for Suze or for Suze's mother. Suze had always been perfectly nice to her, and she seemed to still be a kind woman. There was no reason she shouldn't reproduce as much as she liked.

"I thought you would have had it by now," Jiminy said lamely.

"Maybe a milkshake'll jar it loose," Suze answered goodnaturedly. "Are you here alone?"

It was a reasonable question. Jiminy had shown up at the pool alone; perhaps she was moping all around Fayeville looking for company.

"No, I'm with someone, actually," Jiminy answered. "He's outside."

She motioned toward the door.

"Oooh, a date?" Suze trilled.

Jiminy paused. She shrugged nonchalantly, but couldn't help her smile, much as she knew she should. The rogue smile was all it took.

"It is!" Suze squealed. "Who is he? Someone from here?"

Jiminy mentally kicked herself. She stalled, weighing her options. Should she lie? Downplay? Flaunt? She didn't feel ready for this.

"I don't know if you know him," she hedged.

"We'll find you on our way out," Suze exclaimed, winking and squeezing Jiminy's arm before lumbering off to join her mom at the counter.

As Jiminy walked back, armed with napkins and a fresh uncertainty, she pondered her options. She wasn't sure how Suze would react to her and Bo being together. Perhaps she'd be as mellow and accepting as Cole, but perhaps she wouldn't. Jiminy wondered if she should warn Bo. He was staring at her.

"What's the matter?" he asked.

It bothered her that she was so transparent.

"Nothing," she replied, quickly bending her frown smileward as she brainstormed innocuous explanations. She'd act completely normal with him, no matter what came their way. "I was just thinking of my mom. She used to take me to Dairy Queen for breakfast."

"Sounds like a fantasy mom," Bo replied. "Are you guys close?"

Jiminy shook her head.

"Not really. She sort of checked out when I was still a kid."

"I'm sorry," Bo said sincerely. "Does it bother you to talk about it?"

Before Jiminy could answer, Suze and her mother ambled out into the parking lot. Suze spotted Jiminy and stopped abruptly, looking bewildered. Her mother looked unambiguously disapproving. There were no slug teeth in sight. Just grim, set lip lines.

"I guess that's a yes," Bo said.

Jiminy redirected her attention to him.

"What? No, I don't mind," Jiminy said, a little flustered. "Sorry, I just got distracted by some friends. Do you know Suze Connors?"

Jiminy gestured to where Suze and her mom had been standing, but they were already in their car, pulling out onto the road. Apparently, they didn't always move so slowly.

"Huh," Jiminy said.

"Guess they've got somewhere to be," Bo said wryly.

Jiminy stayed silent, and pained.

"Don't worry about it," Bo continued. "I'm much more interested in you. So what happened with your mom?"

"More like what didn't happen with her," Jiminy replied, still staring at the road. "Not to be dramatic," she continued, shifting her gaze back toward Bo. "It's not a big deal. She had a car accident when I was six. Nothing serious, but she suffered whiplash, so she was given painkillers, and then she got a little too into those."

Bo nodded. It was understandable; he wasn't judging. Jiminy appreciated this.

The accident had at first seemed relatively innocuous—the sort of thing that disrupted a morning but was mainly forgotten by evening, except for lingering insurance implications. But as the painkillers overstayed their welcome, a lot of things began slipping and fraying, sneaking their way toward a permanent shift. Jiminy noticed her mother's dependency on the pills, and was forced to weather the mood swings and the ensuing marital discord. She knew that the day she was sent to the Paint-Your-Own-Pot store at the mall to make something nice for her grandmother was a day of reckoning. Knew when she returned and her father was gone that the day hadn't gone well. Naturally shy to begin with, Jiminy retreated into the role of the awkward, self-absorbed child to avoid having to admit all that she knew to people who would feel obliged to counsel her through it. She learned to be quiet and small, to disappear into backgrounds, to suffocate her sentences before they could betray her. She learned to bottle herself up.

As she folded inward, Jiminy tried to hold fast to her mother. She convinced herself that what her father and everyone else failed to understand was that her mother was finally having fun. A life without pain was a life worth celebrating, with spontaneous dancing and all-night games and endless, shifting plans. It was childhood rediscovered. It was being young at heart. Jiminy understood this. Consistency was a virtue adults overrated so they didn't have to focus on how utterly boring everyday existence was. To gulp all that away and embrace a new reality—how fresh! How rejuvenating! Jiminy opted to go along for the ride, so as not to be left behind.

Eventually, of course, it got even more bumpy and chaotic and unreasonable, and Jiminy was forced to become the adult in the relationship, at far too young an age.

Back in the present day, she wrenched herself away from these tumultuous memories to focus on the moments at hand.

"It wasn't awful," she concluded with a shrug. "My mom and I just kind of switched roles, so I felt like I was taking care of her."

Bo nodded.

"And who was taking care of you?"

"I was taking care of me, too," Jiminy replied. "And luckily, all of that turned me into the confident, take-charge person you see before you today."

Bo laughed, but not unkindly. Jiminy looked directly into his eyes.

"Hey," she said, touching his hand. "Can I ask you something? How big a problem are we going to be?"

Bo stared back at her a moment.

"Tough to tell just yet," he answered slowly. "You game to find out?"

Jiminy nodded.

"You?"

In answer, Bo put his arms around her and pulled her close.

Jiminy remembered what it felt like when her mother had hugged her: like she was a life preserver being clobbered by a drowning woman. Her mom would clutch her tightly, turning her entire world into nothing but dark, fragrant hair. Jiminy and her mother had the same hair, actually, and as Jiminy would breathe in mouthfuls of it, she'd experience the strange sensation of the two of them being tangled up together—unsure of who was who. She'd always had to work to not feel panicked by this.

In contrast, being held by Bo made her feel calm and safe. And as Jiminy looked up at him—into his smooth, handsome face—she was surprised by the sudden instinctive realization that despite everything, this was the happiest she'd ever felt.

———

Lyn remembered the first time she'd laid eyes on Edward, in the fall of 1948, when they were all of sixteen years old. She was visiting relatives a few towns over from Fayeville, walking through an outdoor market, searching for something pretty and cheap for her sister's birthday.

So far, she hadn't found a thing. But rounding the corner of a table full of lucky buckeyes, Lyn stopped suddenly in front of a small booth that she had to lean over to inspect. There were only a few items, but they were gorgeous. Tiny, smooth, impeccable wooden figurines. A horse on its hind legs. A frog mid-leap. A bird taking flight. Little animals in motion, carved out of trees.

Lyn touched them gently with her fingertips. Something about miniatures had always attracted her, perhaps because they belonged to a world she was guaranteed to dominate.

Edward had appeared behind the booth. She hadn't known it was Edward yet, she only knew that he was a tall, serene boy with a lake of a face. One look and she wanted to jump in and drink him up.

She wasn't accustomed to such feelings. She'd never experienced them before. So they scared her, and she stepped back.

"Hello," he'd said.

His voice was clear and friendly, which confused Lyn further. She was more familiar with grumbled asides and downcast eyes.

"You make these?" she'd asked.

She knew that if he said yes, she would have to marry him. She awaited her fate with one arm twisted behind her back, held in place by her other hand.

"I do," he said.

By the time Lyn returned home to St. Louis two weeks later, she had a wooden bird for her sister and a fiancé for herself.

As happened whenever Lyn thought of Edward, the sharp sting of losing him was bound up with the guilt over not being good enough for him when he was alive. She thought of this now, punished herself with it, as she polished Willa's silver, putting each utensil carefully away in the velvet-lined drawer.

Sometimes Lyn thought that Edward knew everything now. That his eternal perch had granted omniscience and he was able to peer around all the corners of their marriage, into all the cracks of their lives. In those moments, she could only hope that he was forgiving. She only hoped that he understood her love. These last many decades, she'd been doing penance to make sure he knew.

And what about their Jiminy? Could she see all, know all, too? Lyn didn't let herself picture this, because her daughter had died too young to understand all the choices that had had to be made, and the necessity of labeling some mistakes "choices."

Jiminy's eyes had been silver-colored. Not the hue of silver that was ripped from the earth and sluiced and smelted and leached and hammered into cold objects that required regular polishing; rather, the tint that revealed itself more naturally: the silver of fish scales flashing, or of the edges of clouds between dusk and dark. Edward used to tell Jiminy that her eyes had dripped from the sky onto her face the night she was born, when the delighted moon had laughed so hard she'd cried. So Jiminy's eyes were moon tears, Edward had declared, as precious and special as her.

Those silver eyes had shimmered with an enthusiasm for life that still made Lyn catch her breath. When she thought of her daughter, and of all the joy she'd embodied, Lyn felt her heart fill. She lost herself in that sensation now, as she wiped a cloth gently along the curve of a serving spoon like it was a tiny brow being soothed.

———

When Willa came home from poker with Jean, Lyn was still polishing, which surprised both of them.

"Lyn? Are you all right?" Willa called as soon as she walked in the door. "Lyn?"

Lyn rubbed harder on a stain as she realized how late it was. Too late to reasonably still be there. She'd been completely lost in memories of Edward and Jiminy, but now here was Willa, to force her back into the present moment.

"I'm in here," Lyn replied.

She didn't stop polishing when Willa entered the room.

"Just trying to get this silver all clean," Lyn said, keeping her head bent over her task.

"It's past ten o'clock," Willa replied. "I was worried when I saw your car. I thought you might've fallen and hurt yourself."

That had happened once, a long time ago, when Lyn had first become old. Carrying some sheets up the stairs, she'd turned her ankle, tumbled, and ended up unconscious at the bottom. Her ankle had recovered, but her back had never been the same.

But there'd been no such accidents this night. To the untrained eye, Lyn appeared to be in one piece.

"Sorry to make you worry," she said.

"Well, no matter," Willa replied. "But why don't you leave this and pick up with it next time. It'll still be here."

Lyn paused but kept her gaze focused downward, on her old, worn-out hands.

"I don't like leaving things unfinished," she said simply.

Willa eyed her carefully, her forehead furrowed in concern.

"Are you all right, Lyn? What's going on?"

Lyn sighed and resumed polishing.

"Just these water stains. But I'm getting 'em. I'm gonna get every last one of 'em."

"I'll get this soon, I swear," Jiminy informed Bo as she struggled to shift the truck into gear.

"I have no doubt," Bo replied. "And then you can drive us to pick up a new transmission."

"Shut up," Jiminy said, smiling. "You're supposed to be helping me. Am I making any improvement?"

"You're showing signs of potential competence," Bo answered.

"I'll try not to let that go to my head."

Bo grinned.

"You're getting better, definitely."

It was true. She'd been able to stutter and glide a little in the high school parking lot. She just needed practice. For Bo's part, he was happy to help her practice all night. Even in light of all the stop-and-start jerking, he couldn't think of a single thing he'd rather be doing.

Which he knew was something his aunt Lyn considered a problem. She hadn't actually said anything to him about his relationship with Jiminy, and Bo hadn't offered an opening for commentary. But he could sense the warning in the way she mentioned the weather turning, or the gas price fluctuation, or his need for a haircut. "You're going places," she seemed to be saying to him beneath these other words. "Don't mess that up."

Abruptly, Bo noticed he was going someplace with considerably fewer jerks and stutters. They were leaving the parking lot, pulling off into the night.

After Lyn finally left, Willa opened all the silverware drawers to take stock. Everything was gleaming. There wasn't a water stain in sight.

Willa hadn't brought any silver into her marriage or received any as wedding presents. She'd never been wealthy enough to afford such things. It had all come after Henry's death, over time, and only because Willa had sifted through hundreds of antique malls over fifty-plus years to procure it. Jean would accompany her on her searches for that one affordable pitcher or ashtray or spoon engraved with someone else's initials, that she'd scoop up and add to her collection.

Willa now owned drawers full of silver. And when it was polished, it didn't matter that it was mismatched and marked by others. It shone, and it was hers.

The only obstacle to her enjoyment of her hard-won silver collection had been Lyn's strong dislike of cleaning it. The polish Willa insisted she use had a powerful chemical stench and gave Lyn a red, painful rash that she'd complained about from the beginning. So for Lyn to voluntarily clean Willa's entire silver collection meant that something was fundamentally wrong. Or, rather, it meant that the thing that was fundamentally wrong had surfaced and announced itself. Willa wondered what it could all lead to as she picked up a cake knife and studied her reflection. In the glare of the overhead light, the whites of her eyes burned back at her.

———

Just south of Fayeville, Interstate 34 sliced through fields and hills, crisscrossing the Allehany River dozens of times. The winding backroads that had existed before the interstate still shadowed it in a twisty, incompetent way, but from the moment it was built, Interstate 34 had been faster, smoother, and straighter.

As soon as I-34 was completed, new restaurants sprang up

near its Fayeville junction. This development, in combination with the grand opening of the HushMart superstore along the access road that led to the interstate, had turned Fayeville's previously bustling Main Street into a neutered, orphaned remnant of another era. It seemed to take no time at all for McDonald's and HushMart to become much more popular than Lucy's Snack Spot or Kurley's Hardware. Even residents who lived within walking distance of the Main Street stores and restaurants no longer just strolled down the block for the things they needed or desired. They were now much more likely to get in their cars and drive toward the interstate instead.

Part of the access road that connected the interstate to Fayeville wasn't as smooth as county officials would have liked. The construction company hired to do the job had failed to adequately take into account the eroding bluff that overhung the planned junction, and as a result, the motorists navigating it were confronted with the added challenge of looking out for falling rocks. Someone from Highway Maintenance was tasked with clearing the rocks out a couple times a week; more frequently when there were storms.

Bo knew about this danger and was prepping Jiminy for the challenge of potentially having to stop and start again, after she had been so happy flying along in fourth gear, slightly too fast for a curvy road.

She was preparing to downshift into third when she was suddenly and instantly blinded.

Bo was, too.

"What the . . . !" he said.

He was exclaiming at the strength and brightness of the light burning into their corneas, but he was also aware that Jiminy wasn't slowing down as planned. He was worried that she might have taken her hands and feet off the controls completely, retracting like a frightened turtle. He couldn't check to ensure this wasn't the case, because he couldn't see anything.

"Brake!" he shouted as they nearly rammed the pickup truck that was assaulting them.

It had come quickly around the curve, safe in the boulder-free lane, with its brights on high, trained on their windshield. It swerved now to avoid them, slowed, and came to a stop.

Bo listened to the sickly crunch of abused machinery as Jiminy brought their own vehicle to an abrupt halt, diagonally across the oncoming lane.

"Reverse!" he shouted, knowing that another car could come around the curve at any moment and slam into his passenger side door. But Jiminy was too shocked to comply.

"Reverse," he said more softly and urgently.

She looked at him for a moment, then struggled with the gear shift. But it seemed that in her startled fright, she'd regressed to square one. She stared down with a look of complete bewilderment. The gear shift might as well have been a cucumber, for all she could remember of what she was supposed to do with it to make this big chunk of metal move for her.

Bo was a calm person, but he knew when he was in real danger. He had a flash of what the pain of impact would feel like, how a life of paralysis would change his plans. He opened his door.

"Scoot over," he commanded.

He slammed his door shut, put a hand on the hood of the truck and launched himself over the front of it, half-sliding, half-scrambling to the other side. His feet landed on the asphalt and he wrenched open the driver's side door to see Jiminy still sitting there, confused.

"Move!" he shouted, helping her roughly along.

"You! Stop right there, boy!" a voice shouted from behind him.

But Bo had seen the glare of headlights on the trees and knew an oncoming car was moments away from their spot, probably driving as fast as they'd been. And now that he'd forced Jiminy into the seat that would receive the impact, he'd be as good as murdering her if he didn't ignore whoever was yelling at him and act quickly.

He slid into the driver's seat, threw the truck into reverse, and jerked them backwards just as an '86 VW Cabriolet veered obliviously around the corner.

It was a car Bo and Jiminy both knew well. As they panted to regain their breath, they watched the Cabriolet screech to a halt to avoid hitting the truck that had caused all the trouble in the first place.

"Sweet Jesus," Lyn exclaimed, as she looked back to make sure it was Bo and Jiminy she thought she'd seen.

It was. And here, too, was Roy Tomlins and his grandson Randy, standing outside yelling while their truck blocked up the road. Lyn couldn't sort these various pieces into an arrangement that helped her understand the scenario she'd stumbled across.

She took a deep breath and opened her door.

"I'm warning you for the last time to get outta that car, boy!" Roy was growling.

He was as old as Lyn, filled with a timeless rage.

"What seems to be the problem?" she asked.

Get out of the car, Bo, she mentally beamed down the road. Though she wasn't positive that this was the best psychic command. If he got out and moved toward them, he'd just be voluntarily coming into range. Perhaps it was better for him to stay in the car, next to the girl. Except for the fact that Roy Tomlins had shouted a direct order that would go unheeded at all of their peril.

"This ain't none a yer bizness," Roy's grandson Randy snarled at Lyn.

Lyn addressed her words to Roy.

"That's my great-nephew, Mr. Tomlins. And Willa Hunt's granddaughter."

Lyn kept her voice submissive. Roy stared hard at her. Something in her tone, or her look, or the sound of the crickets resuming their night song, made him pause in his fury. He stared another beat, then turned and walked toward Bo and Jiminy's car. Lyn hurried after him, struggling to keep up, careful to avoid getting too close.

———————

Inside the car, Jiminy was shaking.

"I'm so sorry, I'm so sorry," she kept repeating.

She was mortified that she'd frozen up. She knew how close they'd come to serious injury, all because of her incompetence. And now these men were yelling at them, and Lyn was there looking worried and beaten down, and Bo had a grimness to his face that Jiminy hadn't seen before. It scared her. He seemed resigned to some kind of disaster.

"I need to get out of the car," Bo said quietly. "But you stay put."

"I don't understand what's happening," she replied, wishing her voice wasn't such a whimper.

"Just stay here," Bo replied. "Just stay here."

She didn't know why they were being shouted at when they were the ones who'd been blinded. She couldn't comprehend how a barely avoided accident seemed to be spiraling toward a worse one. She was bewildered by the unfolding events, whereas Bo seemed to understand exactly what was going on.

Jiminy had an urge to kiss him like she would if he were going off to war. She leaned over to do it, but he gripped her shoulder hard.

"Why are you trying so hard to get us killed?" he said harshly.

He opened his door and got out, leaving Jiminy stunned.

Thank you, Lyn thought to herself. On the walk over, she'd realized that Roy and Randy thought Bo might speed off to escape their wrath, and that they were determined to make sure this didn't occur. Bo wouldn't do that with Lyn there, but she wondered what his reaction would have been otherwise. Lyn knew it was a very good thing she'd come along, and this was a feeling she was unaccustomed to having.

She met Bo's eyes as he stood up straight beside the car, closing the driver's door behind him.

"I toldja stop, boy," Roy said.

"Yes, sir, but I knew another car was coming and we needed to get outta the way in a hurry," Bo replied.

Roy didn't like logic that disagreed with him.

"I toldja stop."

"Sorry, Mr. Tomlins," Bo said. "Hello, Randy."

Bo and Randy had gone to high school together. They'd played on the same football team.

"I'd stay quiet if I was you, Bo," Randy said and scowled.

He was staring past Bo at Jiminy, still seated in the car. He started toward her but was stopped by Bo, who wouldn't step aside. Lyn silently cursed and with her eyes urged her great-nephew to move. The girl was not the one who needed protecting.

"Outta my way, boy," Randy ordered.

Bo hesitated for a moment and locked eyes with his old teammate, grappling with a desire to smash his fist into Randy's face. But feeling his great-aunt's agitation, Bo reluctantly moved aside instead. Randy pushed roughly past him, rapped his knuckles on the car window, and opened the driver's side door.

"You okay?" he asked gruffly.

Jiminy nodded stiffly.

"I'm fine."

"You can speak freely, I won't let anything happen to you," Randy said.

"I'm fine."

"You with this boy willingly?" Roy called.

Lyn sucked air into her lungs. Surely Roy Tomlins didn't think he'd stumbled across a kidnapping. He just didn't like what he saw, and wanted to dress it up in a costume that would offend others, too.

Jiminy looked confused.

"With Bo?" Jiminy said. "Yeah, of course."

This answer didn't bring Lyn any relief, because she observed its impact on Roy and Randy, who were now looking even angrier.

Lyn cut in. "Mr. Tomlins, Bo's been working for Miz Hunt over the summer, and that sometimes involves driving Jiminy places."

As soon as Lyn had started speaking, Roy had put his hand up to block her words, but they'd wended their way through the cracks between his fingers, and now Roy seemed to consider them. Lyn hoped that he would. She recognized that he needed an excuse to back off and leave them alone. She wanted to fashion one for them all.

"That so?" Roy said, turning to Bo. "You working for Miz Hunt?"

Bo nodded. Technically, this was true, though it pained him to play the role his great-aunt was asking him to.

"But she was the one driving," Randy said.

They'd seen them clearly. That was the point of having the brights on in the first place, to reveal what was going on with folks when they thought it was just them. The white girl had been driving, and the black boy had been sitting too close.

"She wanted to learn how to drive stick shift," Bo answered. "Sir."

Lyn's wrinkled nose had told him to add the "sir." She was enlisting different parts of her face to ensure that Bo acted the way he should, each twitch and furrow sending a clear signal, working overtime to keep him out of harm's way.

"And *you* were teaching her?" Roy queried.

Jiminy sat up straighter in the car, looking as though she was just waking from a hazy dream.

"Bo doesn't work for me," she said righteously. "He's my boyfr—"

"He's Miz Hunt's employee," Lyn interrupted.

She was frustrated that her invisible strings didn't reach to this troublemaking girl. Furious that the girl didn't automatically better understand the ways of this place, or what was at stake.

"And our families go way back, as I think you know," Lyn continued. "Miss Jiminy I've known since she was born."

Jiminy gaped at her. Roy looked from one to the other, and then at Bo, who was staring at the ground. In the silence that followed, the crickets grew louder. Roy shifted his weight and rubbed the back of his hand roughly across his nose.

"Just needed to make sure no one was in any kinda trouble," he said finally.

Lyn's insides unclenched. They were going to be okay.

"We weren't till you blinded us," Jiminy retorted. "Your head beams nearly killed us."

Lyn groaned inwardly as Roy's gaze snapped back to the girl. He couldn't believe what he was hearing. Here he'd started out concerned for her, and what did he get in return? Attitude, not gratitude. Though maybe he shouldn't have been surprised, considering she was Willa and Henry's granddaughter. He'd seen her around, he realized now. At Grady's Grill, asking too many questions. She was trouble, that much was for sure.

Roy felt a throbbing in his right temple as he tightened his free hand into a fist. He wanted to teach her a lesson. But what could he do, really? Randy would spring to action with a word, but it was already so late, and Roy was tired. He was ready to move on to the ice cream he was going to eat when he got back home.

"Well, thank goodness no one got hurt," Lyn said cautiously.

Roy squinted at his captive audience, each in turn.

"Y'all watch yourselves," he said, his voice thick with implications for disobedience. "I know plenty of folks who wouldn't be as understandin' as us."

Jiminy, Bo, and Lyn remained silent and motionless as Roy and Randy turned and walked back to their truck. But as their taillights disappeared around the far curve a few moments later, Jiminy burst into tears.

CARLOS CASTAVERDE was trying to think of a seven-letter word for the movement of water across a semi-permeable membrane when his secretary stuck her head through his office doorway.

"Someone to see you."

He nodded without looking up. He knew this answer. He could practically taste the word on the tip of his tongue.

"Mr. Castaverde?"

And away it went. He'd had it and lost it. He sighed and looked up from his crossword, hoping that if the answer still lingered in the air nearby, it would somehow find its way back to him.

Delicate and fresh-looking, the young woman standing in his doorway reminded him of watercress.

Since boyhood, Carlos had been fascinated with plants, and studied them with the religious fervor his parents wished he'd apply to the salvation of his soul. But Carlos didn't care about churches; he cared about field guides, soil acidity, rainfall patterns, and chlorophyll levels. To help him memorize the details of various plant types, he'd begun making instant associations between people he met and plants he already knew. Over time, he'd honed an encyclopedic knowledge of all the major flora, as well as an unshakeable new way of thinking about people.

The watercress woman spoke again.

"Is this a bad time?"

"No, come on in," Carlos replied.

She walked across the room and folded herself into a seat, then stood again, her slender arm outstretched.

"I'm Jiminy Davis," she announced.

"Carlos Casteverde," he replied as he shook her hand. "What can I do for you?"

"I'm from Fayeville, Mississippi," Jiminy said. "Or at least my family is. And something happened there."

Carlos nodded, waiting for her to elaborate. He didn't know exactly where Fayeville was, but the nearest town in Mississippi was a six-hour drive away. The girl had traveled to see him. As busy as he was, he decided to hear her out.

"Something awful. Forty years ago. Like what you've seen and fixed already," she continued.

Carlos had seen and fixed more than he wanted to think about. No one of these buried mysteries was like any of the others, and the last one never prepared him for the next. Practice made him better at uncovering and pursuing, but it never dulled the shock and fury.

"No one seems to know who did it exactly, or if they do, they're not telling. And everyone seems content to just let it lie. But it's not right. And things are all messed up there. I didn't realize it at first, but they are." Jiminy paused.

She stared at the floor for a long moment, then lifted her head to look at Carlos again.

"Things there just aren't the way they're supposed to be," she said.

Carlos watched her closely, trying to remember the last time he'd successfully grown watercress. It was the kind of thing best stumbled upon in nature, floating thick in a cold, shallow stream.

"I'll need to learn a lot more," he replied as his crossword answer came to him, permeating the membrane of his forgetfulness at last.

Osmosis. Of course.

––––––––––

An hour later, Jiminy had shown Carlos the notes she'd made on everything to date, along with the photocopied clippings from the *Ledger* and her grandfather's diary. She'd explained the circumstances of Edward's and Jiminy's deaths, and relayed the stories from the county pool and Grady's Grill and the stretch of highway near Falling Rock Curve. Carlos had looked at and listened to it all, and now Jiminy was waiting to see how well she'd done.

As she waited, she stared at his cheekbones, following their slant down toward a mouth that was set in a thinking frown. She noted for the second time that Carlos looked like somebody famous who was trying to go unrecognized, though she couldn't place her finger on exactly who. It was something about his eyebrows and cheeks, something Native American to the shape of his features. She felt she'd seen him in a western, or a cop show.

He certainly wasn't dressed to be noticed. Jiminy wondered if he changed out of his jeans and flannel shirt on the days he went to court. There wasn't anything scruffy about him—he was all clean lines and smooth shaves—but he wasn't scrubbed. And if she hadn't researched him and learned that he was forty-four years old, she wouldn't have been able to tell his age. She'd have guessed anywhere from thirty to fifty. Older than her, but perhaps not significantly.

If Carlos didn't help her, she wasn't sure what she'd do. She was determined to prove some things, but she didn't have the expertise and resources to pursue the unsolved Waters case on her own. She'd begun the fieldwork, but she needed Carlos in order to make something of it. And in making something of it, she hoped to make something of herself.

Carlos tapped the eraser of his pencil against his temple. He opened up a large, flat, tan book. He glanced up at Jiminy's entreating gaze.

"I can be in Fayeville next Tuesday," he said.

S HE WAS DETERMINED to meet with him, even though he works out of Texarkana," Willa told Jean between huffs as she sliced her remote control racket through the air.

Willa was improving rapidly at virtual tennis, a game to which Jean had only recently introduced her. After their last trip to Trudi's Tresses, Jean had insisted Willa come into the house when she dropped her off. She'd pulled Willa eagerly up her walk, in the exact way that she'd been pulling her into dances and kitchens, parties and quiet confidences, for nearly seventy years. The gesture made them feel young.

Willa had only offered enough resistance to Jean's tugging to make it more insistent. When they reached the living room, Jean had pointed to a small white box in front of her TV screen.

"Ta da!" she exclaimed.

"What is it?" Willa asked.

"Our new tennis court!" Jean exclaimed excitedly. "Stand there. Are you limber?"

This wasn't the first time Jean had asked her this. She'd tried to get Willa into yoga several years ago without any luck.

"You know I'm not," Willa replied.

"Just stay there," Jean instructed, handing Willa an oddly shaped remote control. "You'll see how it works."

Before them, the TV screen had changed to an image of a tennis court with two figures squared off against each other across the net.

"I'm the one with the dark hair," Jean informed Willa, indicating the brunette on the screen. "And you're the blonde. I'm serving, so just watch the screen, and when the ball comes to you, pretend your remote is a tennis racket and hit it back to me."

"What do you mean hit it back to you? There's nothing to hit back," Willa replied.

"Just watch," Jean ordered.

She made sure Willa was watching both her and the TV, then pressed the button that would release the on-screen ball and, holding the remote firmly in her hand, sliced her arm through the air in a serving motion. On the screen, her player served perfectly to Willa's character, who stayed completely still as the ball passed her by.

"Hit it!" Jean cried.

"Hit what?" Willa demanded, confused.

"On the screen, don't look away from the screen!"

"I got distracted by your little dance."

"Okay, just look at the real me for a second," Jean said and sighed. "See, I'm treating the remote like my racket. This is the way I serve, this is my forehand, this is my backhand."

Willa watched Jean demonstrate each of these, pantomiming tennis, playing against the air.

"Now everything I just did, I'm going to repeat, but this time don't look at me. Look at the TV instead."

Willa watched the screen and saw the dark-haired tennis player in the short skirt make a serving stroke, a forehand, and a backhand.

"Oh," Willa said, a note of dawning comprehension in her voice.

"You got it?"

"Hang on."

Keeping her eyes glued to the blond on the screen, Willa made a few forehand strokes. The blond tennis player did, too.

"Oh!" Willa cried, with significantly more delight.

Before long, they were enjoying long rallies. They weren't the quickest of athletes, but they were steady and dedicated, and they'd begun playing once a week. It was the first time they'd regularly raised their heartbeats in over a decade.

"So this Carlos fella knew Emmet Till?" Jean asked, panting.

"No, no," Willa batted this away. "The Emmet Till Act. It's a government thing. He works with it somehow, and he opens up old unsolved cases, and investigates them. Jiminy read all about him."

This wasn't as foreign to Jean as her reactions would imply. She'd reviewed some of Jiminy's Google searches by using the "History" tab on her computer and had followed a few of the links. Still, Jean hadn't fully engaged with what she'd discovered. She hadn't wanted to get pulled back in.

She was getting pulled back in now, though. It appeared that all of them might be.

"She drove all the way to Texarkana? That's seven hours from here."

Jean tried to catch Willa off guard with a forehand to the left back corner of the virtual court. Willa stretched to return it.

"As I said, she was determined," Willa replied, energized to have made the shot.

Jean was getting frustrated. She was glad that their games had become more competitive, but she was accustomed to winning more easily.

"And she went by herself?" she asked.

Which was the polite way of asking whether Bo went with her; whether they were spending the night together someplace in a strange town.

"Yes. By herself," Willa replied with her lips pursed.

Willa was still in disbelief that her granddaughter had ever taken up with Bo. Though by the time Jiminy confirmed the relationship, late at night after the Roy Tomlins run-in, the two were freshly broken up.

"Bo doesn't think we should see each other anymore," Jiminy had said.

In a detached tone, she'd relayed the story of the encounter with Roy and Randy, and of the strange, sad way it had impacted Bo. He had sat in silence during the slow drive back to Willa's farm. He parked the truck and climbed out and stood in the darkness on the gravel driveway, staring up at the sky. Jiminy had collected herself and joined him, reaching out for his hand. Which is when he began to speak in a voice one husky octave off of normal. He explained that Jiminy just fundamentally couldn't understand what they were up against in Fayeville. He called himself stupid for thinking there was a chance they'd be let alone, and said he couldn't in good conscience continue putting her at risk. He said that under different circumstances he'd be willing to force the issue, but the reality was that the summer was ending and neither of them planned to stay in town much longer. Given that, he didn't think it was wise for them to make everything more difficult and dangerous than it needed to be. He'd focus on his studying, and she'd figure out her next steps. Down the line, maybe their paths could cross again in some friendlier, easier place.

Jiminy had been unable to reply except to shake her head no while rogue tears slipped from the corners of her eyes. Bo took her hand, kissed her cheek, and told her it was better for them both if they just didn't see each other anymore. And then he left.

Willa had listened to her granddaughter, wishing she could

alleviate her hurt. But she lacked confidence in her caretaking skills. She'd already failed spectacularly with Jiminy's mother, as far as she could tell. And her timid attempts to help out with Jiminy when her daughter was otherwise engaged had been mainly rebuffed. Beyond agreeing to a handful of sporadic visits, Margaret had made a point of letting Willa know that her services were not needed. So Willa had backed off. But now Jiminy was on her own and had sought Willa out. Was she being given another chance? She'd tried her hardest to be comforting and wise.

"I know it doesn't seem like it, but Bo's right," she'd said. "This is for the best."

To Willa's surprise, Jiminy had been outraged instead of soothed.

"How could you say that?" she demanded.

"It's not right, I know, but this isn't a battle worth fighting right now. Listen to Bo. When a young person is trying to make something of themselves, they should avoid unnecessary distractions that might throw them off course."

Jiminy blanched. She brought her hand down to the table.

"Bo isn't a distraction, he's an inspiration!"

Willa looked at her granddaughter with a face full of sympathy and apology. But it was an apology for what she was about to say rather than what she already had.

"I know," she explained gently. "I was talking about you."

Jiminy sat there, stunned, for a very long moment, and then she burst out laughing. It had taken Willa a few seconds to determine that it was laughter and not sobs.

"I get it, I'm the distraction," Jiminy replied. "Bo's the one actually making something of himself, and I'm the one getting him off track. Of course. You're absolutely right."

The next morning, Jiminy had told Willa that she was headed to Texarkana, and might be gone a few days.

"Does Lyn know what she's up to?" Jean asked Willa, determined to win the game in the next few strokes.

They were both getting tired, and Jean was trying to capitalize on any mistakes Willa might make.

"Because I imagine Lyn must have some strong feelings about it," she continued. "I imagine she just might want it left alone."

"I'm leaving that between Jiminy and Lyn," Willa answered, feeling a burn in her right side as she reached to return a shot that barely cleared the net.

"But don't you think Lyn would prefer Jiminy to leave all this alone?" Jean repeated, taking advantage of the weak return to hurtle a shot over the head of Willa's avatar, to the opposite corner of the virtual court.

Willa didn't even try to go for it. Instead, she dropped her arm to her side and turned to face Jean.

"I don't know," she answered in exasperation. "Is that what *you'd* prefer?"

Part Two

I N T H E G R A N D R O O M of his plantation mansion ten miles
outside of Fayeville, Travis Brayer was profoundly irri-
tated.

He'd decided to watch *The Apartment* after reading that his
favorite director watched it before beginning any major project. It so happened that Travis had a major project to begin, so
he'd put in *The Apartment* with high expectations. And now he
was trying to figure out if he'd misunderstood and whether
there might be another movie of the same name.

He supposed the plot had been amusing enough, but Bud
Baxter was such a loser—not remotely the type of character to
inspire anyone to spearhead an ambitious new project. Travis
overturned his tray in disgust.

"Now, Mr. Brayer, what are you doing?" the nurse asked as
she hustled in to pick up the mess. "If you don't want any more
juice, you can just tell me and I'll take this away. No need to
make a scene."

Travis ignored her. He remembered the days when the help
had been frightened of him, and he deeply resented the fact
that this no longer seemed to be the case. How and when had
he lost his authority?

"Mr. Bobby should be showing up soon," the nurse said.

If he took this news well, she might pass over his stack of
phone messages, but she needed to determine the degree of
his lucidity first. Outbursts could signal movement in either
direction.

"That's State Senator Brayer to you," Travis replied shortly.

He was lucid enough, and prickly as ever. The nurse decided

to hang on to his messages a bit longer. He'd never know the difference, after all.

"Yes, sir, that's the one," she answered. "The future governor."

She mopped up the spilled juice with a washcloth and took the tray with her on her way out of the room, just as the dogs began barking from the front porch.

"Dad?" Bobby called soon after from the marble foyer.

"He's in his study," Travis heard the nurse instruct.

A moment later, Bobby stood before him.

"Hi, Dad, how ya feeling?" Bobby asked.

He bent over to shake the old man's hand. The two of them didn't kiss or embrace. They never had, and now that Travis was increasingly fragile, his son was grateful for their more formal routine.

"Like I'm running out of time," Travis answered with uncharacteristic candor. "I want to get my memoirs done faster than my brain and hands will let me."

Bobby nodded and smiled his practiced, understanding state-senator smile.

"Why don't you let me get someone to help you?" he offered.

The people Bobby got to help his father were trained and efficient, and irksomely controlling. Travis had put up with their influx to this point because they were necessary, but he was beginning to feel that enough was enough.

"This is something I've got to do on my own," he answered firmly.

Again, Bobby nodded empathetically.

"I completely understand, Dad. No one but you *could* do it. But you could have some helpers. You'd still be the one doing all the real work, but instead of having to write everything out, you could dictate. Other people could go through all those boxes of old material and bring the most important stuff to you. Think about it."

Travis decided he would. The act of bossing people around had always appealed to him, which his son knew as well as anybody. Plus, it really couldn't be denied that he'd work at a faster pace with some assistance. But he detected self-interest in his son's suggestion, and this gave him pause.

"Maybe I will get some help," Travis conceded. "Roy and the others have grandkids always looking for summer money—I'll get some of them to pitch in."

As suspected, Bobby Brayer greeted this solution with dismay.

"They won't do as good a job as a skilled typist and researcher. I'll get you someone, Dad. I'll arrange the whole thing."

Travis bet he would. He'd arrange it so that whatever Bobby wanted in or out of Travis's memoirs would be controlled by this new employee. His son didn't play straight and fair like a man should. He'd inherited his mother's gift for manipulation. Travis was on to him.

"You understand I'm gonna write this book the way I want," Travis said, taking the stern tone with his son that he'd perfected over forty years.

"Of course," Bobby answered. "I'm just trying to help."

Travis grunted.

"Isn't everyone taking good care of you here?" Bobby pressed.

Travis grunted again.

His body was failing him by the day, and he could only hope that his mind wouldn't follow suit. He'd lost his ability to walk, to relieve himself, even to breathe for long periods of time without a respirator. A small army of caretakers swarmed around him to keep him stretched and fed and alive, and he supposed he was grateful for this. He didn't allow himself to consider the fact that he was actually dying. He kept thinking of old age as the flu—an illness he'd forgotten to inoculate against, but that he could recover from with enough rest and fluids. He honestly expected to wake up one morning a little bit younger than the day before, the first sign that he was on the road to recovery. Toward this end, he drank his juices and did his exercises and bore the indignities of being changed and washed by strangers. It was all temporary. He'd be on the mend soon enough.

"How's the campaign going?" Travis asked.

Bobby looked out the window, past the orchard to the far-off pastures that rolled down to the river's edge.

"We're ten points down, but gaining," he answered. "I need to cut another commercial, which is something I wanted to talk to you about."

Travis nodded expectantly. He'd never been on television before, but he'd always believed he should be. Now it seemed his debut might be imminent.

"Would it be all right if I shot one here?" Bobby asked.

As he took a long pause to make it seem like he was considering the request, Travis reflected that it was too bad they couldn't have filmed this commercial a few years ago, when he might've showcased his cattle-wrangling or tree-chopping skills. Travis used to engage in all kinds of manly, athletic activities, before his aging had telescoped his days into their current narrow confines. But he still felt capable of projecting a unique toughness, and he looked forward to the opportunity to impress a larger audience.

"I think that'd be fine," he answered.

"Great, thanks. We'll stay outside, totally out of your way.

You won't even know we're here, I promise. It'll take a full day, but if all goes well, you won't hear a thing."

"You don't want me in it?" Travis asked incredulously.

Bobby hadn't anticipated his father's hurt.

"You're in most of them already," he replied. "They use those photos of me when I was younger, with you and Mother. You've seen them, you look great in them."

Old photos, of course. Mug shots of better times, when Travis was revered, and sought after. This was clearly no longer the case. Other people were now firmly in charge, and the pain of this was brutal.

———

Rosa Gonzalez had worked a long, exhausting day in the hot Tortillas kitchen, after a sleepless night in which the baby had screamed every hour and a half. As the sun was setting, she finally stopped for a break. She escaped the heat of the kitchen to sit outside in one of her pretty new chairs and watch swallows swoop and swerve in plague-proportion swarms. She marveled at their synchronized, undulating waves and imagined she was at some kind of avian ocean's edge.

Two trucks pulled up and broke her reverie. She didn't recognize them, which was rare. Tortillas catered primarily to the Latino community within Fayeville. It wasn't often that others wandered in, although Rosa assumed it would just take time to convince the rest of the town to give them a try. She knew her food was good. In America, all you needed was to be good and work hard, and success would follow. This is what she firmly believed.

Five young men piled out of the trucks, two out of the first, three from the second. They had tattoos and buzz cuts and looked like they hadn't yet reached their twenties. Rosa briefly wondered if they might be soldiers since she knew that lots of young Fayeville men signed up for the armed forces. But there was an undisciplined air about this particular group that made her reconsider. She didn't really care who they were or where they came from. If they were hungry, she would feed them.

Or she'd get Juan to feed them. She wasn't quite recovered. She stayed seated, but greeted them with a smile.

"Hello!" she said brightly. "Welcome to Tortillas!"

She and Juan had argued about whether to give in to the erroneous local pronunciation of the name or to insist on the correct version. Rosa had advocated assimilation, saying it didn't really matter and that they'd get more business if they didn't turn people off by making them think they couldn't talk right. Juan had insisted they pronounce it the way it was supposed to be pronounced. He assured her people would come around, that they might even enjoy learning a bit of Spanish.

"Tor-tee-yas?" one of the young men repeated. "What's that mean?"

He had a tattoo of a bull with longhorns on his right upper bicep.

"They're a little like thin pancakes, made with corn or flour. We make them with corn. You wrap chicken or beef in them. They're delicious! Come inside and try."

Whenever she had to explain what tortillas were to people, she felt secretly sorry for them, like they were sheltered children who'd been deprived of very basic knowledge available to everyone else. And sometimes she found people's ignorance disingenuous. Who hadn't heard of a tortilla, in this day and age? Still, she had to stay polite.

"They're a little bit like hot dog buns, but for Mexican food," Rosa continued, determined to connect with these potential new patrons. "Did you know hot dog vendors used to give people gloves to eat their hot dogs with to avoid burned hands? But people kept stealing the gloves, so one hot dog seller asked his friend, who was a baker, if he would bake some kind of edible glove that they could use instead. And his friend came up with the hot dog bun! *Interesante*, no?"

Rosa didn't catch herself in time. She blushed.

"I mean, that's interesting, right, guys?"

The young men were staring at her. They didn't seem to find it that interesting. Rosa hoped they would just move inside so Juan could handle them. She didn't want to talk any more.

"We're not here for your dirty buns," the smallest one said.

The others snickered. The one with the longhorn tattoo high-fived the small one. Rosa kept her mouth closed. She tugged her skirt down to make sure it was reaching to her calf.

"You feel like you're sitting pretty, doncha?" the one with the curly blond hair asked her.

His tattoo was a tractor with angel wings, on a part of his chest she could see because he was wearing a tank top.

"Everything's lookin' pretty good for you from there, ain't it? You got yourself a regular catbird seat."

"What's a catbird seat?" the one with the longhorn tattoo asked.

The blond-haired man ignored him, so he turned to the small one.

"Seriously, what is it?" he asked in a low voice.

The small guy shook his head in a way meant to convey that his friend was an idiot for asking, as well as suggest that he knew the answer, when he actually didn't. Rosa was able to discern all of this even as she sat perfectly still in fear, wondering when Juan would come out to check on her.

"Didja hear me, Mex?" the one with curly blond hair asked.

Rosa pretended this was a friendly nickname. She didn't smile, but she looked alert.

"I don't know what you mean," she said softly.

"Gittup," the small guy suddenly bellowed. "Gittup-offa-those."

Rosa wasn't sure what he was saying, he was speaking too quickly and loudly. She understood English perfectly well, but she couldn't comprehend this kind of quick rage. He took a step toward her.

"What's going on?" Juan called from the porch.

Rosa felt a surge of gratitude. She knew the danger hadn't passed, but simply having Juan with her made things better. And at least there would be a witness.

"Those chairs don't belong to you," the one with blond hair said to Juan.

"Rosa, why don't you come inside," Juan said quietly.

Rosa hurried to her feet and skirted around the men. She climbed the porch and touched Juan's arm as she passed him. Juan was taller than the small one, but he wasn't a large man. Rosa heard him close the porch door behind her, and she murmured prayers in rapid Spanish as she ran to their baby, tortured by the suspicion that they were utterly on their own.

————

Grady was wiping down his counter and thinking about a news show that had informed him that most people's kitchen sinks were sixty times dirtier than their toilets when the bell on the diner door jingled.

"Sorry, closed until tomorrow," he said without looking up.

"Just wanted to let you know we got the Brayer chairs back."

It was Roy's grandson saying this from the doorway. The curly blond-headed one named Randy who used to shoot spitballs out of straws when he'd come to eat at the Grill. Grady had spent a lot of time cleaning up after him. He'd grown up, but not too much.

"That so," Grady answered.

He stopped wiping and walked outside. The chairs were there all right, in the back of Randy's truck, standing straight up like they were arranged for a traveling dinner party.

Grady reprimanded him. "You gotta lay 'em down so they don't get blown over."

He wondered why some people didn't have more natural sense. He felt it was a generational deficiency. These younger boys weren't skilled at manual labor and seemed incapable of the simplest tasks. They might be better with computers and cell phones, but they were lesser men. Grady had made his own kids learn how to change tires and locks, how to build and fix. Just basic skills that were dying out, it seemed to him. Grown-up kids these days thought they could hire someone else to handle such things, but they weren't spending their saved time in any kind of productive, worthwhile way. It was a shame.

Whether or not Grady realized it, his annoyance actually sprang from the fact that the sight of the chairs in the truck meant they'd been forcibly taken from outside Tortillas, and this upset him. He'd gone along with the plan because it had been the only thing to do, but he'd secretly hoped that it wouldn't be enacted. He felt guilty for having been the initiating force to begin with, and he'd been hoping that everyone would get distracted by something else for long enough to just forget about the chairs. He recognized the delusional aspect of this thinking, and it only served to aggravate him further.

Grady watched Roy's grandson struggle to rearrange the chairs, before stepping in to show him how to do it. A couple of the other boys climbed out of the truck cab to assist.

So basic. Grady shuddered to contemplate what else they were screwing up. He cleared his throat.

"Was there any trouble getting these?" he asked.

Randy grinned in a way that made Grady's stomach turn.

"Nothing we couldn't handle," he answered.

Still, Grady hoped it was just big talk. He nodded.

"Good to hear."

Only when the truck was driving away did Grady see Juan standing, stopped in his tracks, staring. How long he'd been there, Grady didn't know, though it seemed evident by his expression that it had at least been long enough to register that Grady was friendly with the gang of men who'd obviously caused him trouble. Juan's clothes were dirty and his lip bloodied. Grady's heart sank.

"Juan," he said.

They'd talked about how "Juan" was Spanish for "John," which was Grady's son's name. Grady had shown him Christmas cards, and the spot on the map where John lived. Juan had mentioned that he had relatives in California, too.

Juan didn't respond to Grady. He stood there, holding his hand to his split lip, for another long moment.

"I didn't know they were gonna do that, Juan," Grady said.

He heard how unconvincing he sounded. He was aware that even he didn't believe himself. Juan turned and walked away.

"I'm sorry," Grady called to his back.

Back at his sink, later, Grady stared at the sponge in his hand. He imagined he could feel bacteria oozing out of it, covering him like flies on a carcass.

———

One of Willa's least favorite chores was a weekly necessity. She didn't mind collecting the trash from her own home and bagging it all up for disposal. But mixing it in with the refuse of the larger town was another matter altogether. The smell of the dump overwhelmed her, particularly on hot summer days. Since Jiminy arrived, Willa had tasked her with taking the garbage there, feeling only mildly guilty that she was subjecting her granddaughter to the ordeal. She reminded herself that Jiminy was young and hardy. She could take it.

Jiminy didn't love the assignment, but she did it without complaint. Standing beside the open trunk of Willa's car, she tossed three bulging bags of garbage one by one, up and over the Dumpster's high metal wall. As she listened to the thuds of their landings, she was suddenly struck by how hollow she felt with Bo gone from her life. But she was filling up with other things, she told herself. It was important that she keep moving.

She turned to slam the trunk shut and felt something brush against her leg. The perpetrator, a gray kitten with two different-colored eyes, doubled back for more contact. Jiminy's grandmother had warned her that people used the dump to dispose of unwanted animals, and Jiminy had previously encountered the pack of feral dogs that roamed the nearby fields. She assumed this kitten had to be a recent arrival based on the fact that it was still alive.

One of the kitten's eyes was brown, the other blue. The effect was disconcerting. Looking into its face, Jiminy felt for a second that she was being hypnotized. Later, she decided this might have been the reason she scooped up the kitten and put it in the seat next to her before driving off. She couldn't account for it otherwise. She knew her grandmother wouldn't allow her to keep it.

Before getting back on the main road, Jiminy stopped at a nearby hill, grabbed her backpack, and trekked to the top. The kitten followed her closely, picking its way through the long grass. Under a crabapple tree, Jiminy settled in the shade and looked down toward the river. The kitten climbed into her lap.

"Where'd you come from?" she asked it, wondering whether it was really as healthy as it appeared. The dump had to be an incubator for all kinds of disease.

"Maybe I'll call you Cholera," Jiminy said.

The kitten turned over and rubbed its chin on her hand.

In Jiminy's opinion, Cholera was the most lyrically named of the deadly diseases. Jiminy opened her bag and took out her grandfather's diary, along with another book her grandmother had given her upon her return from Texarkana. It was an old ledger detailing the business details of Henry Hunt's Carpentry. Willa hadn't said much when she handed it over, just that she hoped it might help.

The kitten was now purring in the grass beside Jiminy's leg, a furry little motor humming against her skin. Jiminy was envious of how little it had taken for the creature to attain a level of contentment that caused it to physically vibrate. She found this amazing.

She flipped open the ledger, which appeared to be a fairly straightforward account of the woodworking business run by Henry and Edward. They'd sold handcrafted cradles, cabinets, beds, bureaus, doors, chairs, tables, and shelves in the first year alone. Jiminy knew that Edward had been the craftsman and her grandfather the sales agent, but this breakdown wasn't reflected in the ledger. Along the left-hand side of the page was a list of all the paying customers, along with what they'd purchased and how they'd paid. Jiminy recognized many of the names. The Hatcherts had ordered a hand-carved chessboard. The Brayers had commissioned a table and chairs. The Connors had paid for a decorated front gate. All kinds of orders had been accepted, large and small.

After checking out each and every entry in the ledger, Jiminy turned her attention once more to her grandpa's diary. With Carlos due to arrive in two days, she wanted to revisit all that she already knew. She wanted to feel as prepared as possible.

Looking at the June 24, 1966, entry gave her chills, just as it had before. "Edward and Jiminy found, buried." Now that she knew more, she could better imagine how distraught her grandfather must have been as he'd written this. Henry and Edward had grown up together. They'd worked side by side in the carpentry business and on the farm, along with their wives and daughters. They'd been as close as family, according to Walton Trawler. The rest of Fayeville had apparently looked askance at the intimacy of their relationship, but that hadn't stopped them from living their lives on their own terms. Only untimely death had stopped this, inflicted by a hatred that hunted and stalked and, finally, brutally pounced. What a world where that happened. Jiminy felt a searing anguish flash through her chest. She shut the diary and sank into the grass, laying her arm across her eyes to block the glare. There were times in her life, and this was one of them, when she wished she could just grow straight into the ground.

WILLA KNELT ON HER KNEES by her bed, aware that this would be the proper position to take if she prayed. It was also the best position for fishing something out from underneath her mattress. She rooted around for a moment, grateful that she still had the flexibility for such a maneuver, and conscious that she was more than a little sore from her virtual tennis matches. Her hand finally found its target, which she slowly extracted.

She hadn't looked at the album in years and she'd never shown it to anyone else. But now that Jiminy had brought Carlos here, and they were prying into what Willa had previously thought might stay buried forever, it seemed important to share its contents.

Henry had taken all the photos in the album, so when Willa looked at them, she imagined seeing the subjects live, from his perspective. There was a shot of Edward with a whittling knife. There was a shot of the house, which Henry and Edward had built by themselves. There was the big rock by the river, where they'd lain in the sun, warming themselves after plunges into the cold water. She imagined Henry capturing these moments in his careful way, determined to memorialize the people and places he loved best.

There was a photo of her, pregnant, with her arms around her stomach, standing in the kitchen doorway. Behind her was Lyn, rolling something on the counter. Biscuit dough, most likely. They'd always eaten a lot of biscuits, but Willa had craved them incessantly when she was pregnant. Willa was ostensibly the focus of the photo, featured in the center, but she'd come out slightly fuzzy. It was Lyn whose profile was sharp and clear. She wasn't looking at the camera, but she was still turned slightly toward it, illuminated by the sunlight streaming in through the kitchen window. Covered in a fine dusting of flour, she looked like an angel.

What had Henry seen when he'd looked through that lens?

Because Willa was in the middle of it, he'd certainly seen a wife. One that he'd loved in a quiet, deliberate way. Willa had adored him, particularly in the early years of their marriage. And Henry had made her feel, if not adored, then certainly cherished, which had seemed permanent and holy.

And when he'd looked at Lyn, consciously or subconsciously focused on Lyn? He'd also seen a wife, certainly. The wife of his employee, partner, and friend. He'd seen a tenant and a servant and a parent. Willa couldn't be sure what else Henry had seen in that moment. She'd never fully understood it, especially back then.

The only thing that had seemed certain was that Henry didn't care for Lyn, which had always distressed Willa. Henry had mentioned early on in their marriage that he felt Edward had made a bad match. By that point, Edward and Lyn had already been married for years and were raising their daughter in the little house on the edge of the farm. Willa had liked Lyn immediately and was touched by how deeply Lyn and Edward evidently loved each other. Their affection was a palpable thing, something that sat alongside them in the room, constantly present. Because of this, Willa had argued with Henry when he'd made his "bad match" comment. She'd spoken up for Lyn, defended her, said she seemed like a very good wife.

But Henry had shook his head and told her sharply not to feel such familiarity. Not to feel such familiarity! They were closer with the Waters family than they were with anyone else, including relatives. But she'd stayed quiet, sensing that for some reason Henry needed to feel this way, and that she needed to let him. She'd bit her tongue when Henry had suggested Lyn spend her workdays elsewhere, and missed her silently when Lyn found employment at Brayer Plantation. But Willa had felt strongly all along that Lyn belonged with them on the farm. If only Henry had let her be.

Willa and Henry had tried for a baby for five years before they had their daughter. So when Henry was looking through the lens of his camera, partly at his pregnant wife and partly at a woman he couldn't stand, was he feeling victorious? Or finally trapped?

The photos at the very end of the album were not pleasant to look at. They were in a separate envelope, tucked into a pocket on the inside of the back cover. The ones of the bodies were understandably gruesome, but even the still shots of the survivors had a pathos that repelled the eye. Some grief draws people in, but the kind Henry had captured was as harsh as a flashing hazard light. One look told a viewer it was best to steer clear.

Willa forced herself to look at the photos of Edward and Jiminy for a full second. They were battered. They didn't look like themselves, much less each other, which was always the thing Willa naturally looked for. She wished she had more photos of them unharmed and alive, to help her shape happier memories.

She moved on to the others. There was her daughter standing on the porch, holding a kitten. Willa hadn't let her keep the kitten in the house. She'd banished it to the barn, and it wasn't long before it disappeared. It was still alive in this photograph, but her daughter's seven-year-old face was creased and crinkled in concern. She looked precious and wounded, and this was what made Willa question her assumption that she'd been oblivious and resilient. This was the evidence that proved her wrong— that showed a soul in quiet crisis. Had Henry left it for her, to help her know their daughter better, as a parting gift?

The next photo was of Lyn, the only one Willa had ever seen that was taken with Lyn's knowledge and presumed cooperation. In any of the others, Lyn was always in the background or on the periphery, engaged in some other task, unattuned to the camera's presence. But in this one, she was facing the lens head-on, aware exactly of what was going on.

She was wearing an old overcoat that had belonged to Edward. She was simply standing, arms at her side, staring into the camera. And her face was blank. There was no evident emotion— no fury or sadness or irritation. None of the tension that usually appeared when she was in close proximity to Henry. In its place was a hollowness that hinted at a level of pain unknown to most. Her whole presence gave the impression that her heart had an open wound.

The last photograph in this final group was a self-portrait of Henry. Henry never let anyone else touch his camera, so he must've set the camera on some surface across from him. It had been cold out, to judge by the flush in his cheeks and at the tip of his nose. He, too, stared straight into the camera, unsmiling, a questioning expression on his prematurely aged face. He looked as though he'd just asked the camera something and had been waiting, hoping, for an answer. And that the timer had gone off at the exact second he'd realized he wasn't going to get one.

Willa stared at this last photo the longest, her head filled with her own questions. In the final round of pictures Henry shot before he died, he hadn't taken one of her. Was this because they were all for her? Had he intended her to be the viewer, and thus purposely trained his camera on those she'd need to understand? Willa wanted to think of it this way. She didn't want to contemplate the alternative, that she just hadn't made his final cut. That none of the moments he'd felt compelled to capture and memorialize had involved her.

Of course he hadn't known he was going to die. Maybe she'd been next on his list.

L YN GAZED ACROSS her kitchen table at the stranger sitting calmly in one of the chairs that Edward had carved. Jiminy hovered nearby, leaning in and out of the doorway like she was caught up in a current. The sheaf of onionskin paper lay on the table, flimsy against the wood.

"Do you recognize that report?" the man asked Lyn.

His name was Carlos, Lyn knew, and he was from Texas. Willa's granddaughter had explained why she'd wanted to get him involved, touting his history of successful prosecution of unsolved civil rights crimes. Before the run-in with Roy and Randy Tomlins near the interstate junction, Lyn never would have been persuaded to cooperate. But that night had proven that the hatred that had stolen her husband and daughter was now actively threatening another loved one in the here and now. It wasn't just about Lyn and her painful past. It was now about Bo—who looked so much like Edward—and a still-forming future. As the force of that realization struck her, Lyn had felt something stirring within, almost as though she was shifting out of neutral and into gear. She'd understood clearly that what had happened so long ago lived on, and she'd suddenly decided that she'd be damned if it outlived her. For the first time in forty years, she'd felt a compelling reason to stick around.

"No, I never saw this," Lyn answered.

"Does it seem accurate, though?"

Lyn looked again at the first page of the onionskin pile. It was a yellowed transcript of her visit to the police station on June 24, 1966. She'd gone in two weeks previous to this visit in order to report that her husband and daughter were missing, but she'd been told that they'd probably just run off without her, and that it wasn't the practice of the Fayeville sheriff's office to get caught up in domestic disagreements.

Fourteen days later, the bodies of Edward and Jiminy were found, and Lyn returned to report their murder. The sheriff was dismissive, telling her that he didn't have resources to waste on a silly woman's delusions. According to him, it seemed likely that Edward and Jiminy had stopped to cool off in the river and gotten in over their heads. They didn't know how to swim that well, did they? Did they? He pressed Lyn. He raised his voice to intimidate her, suggesting with his jabbing finger that she might be getting in over her head herself.

Lyn had stayed very calm and pointed out that bruises and bullet wounds suggested something other than drowning. She said they had been driving home from a town upstate, and someone had run them down and killed them. But the sheriff waved her off, lamenting her "overhyperactive imagination."

Lyn remembered all this as she read the transcript in front of her:

> Lyn Waters made unsubstantiated claim that her husband, Edward Waters, and her daughter, Jiminy Waters, were murdered. All evidence points to accidental drowning. No charges will be filed.

Lyn looked up at the man across her table.

"Does it seem accurate?" she repeated. "That's what you asked?"

"I meant, does it accurately describe their attitude. Did you try to talk to the sheriff and was he that dismissive."

"Yes," Lyn answered.

Carlos nodded. Lyn reminded him of an olive tree, stately and gnarled. He was used to the resignation she emanated. He had seen her brand of empty expression on others, in previous cases. So much of the time the surviving relatives he encountered seemed defined less by the presence of ongoing life than by the absence of loved ones whose lives were cut too short.

"Do you remember it well? Do you mind talking about it?"

Lyn looked past him at Willa's granddaughter, who stared back, suddenly self-conscious.

"I'll just wait outside," she said, slipping out the screen door.

Lyn was glad of this. She didn't want her around while she talked about the real Jiminy.

"You have something against her?" Carlos asked.

His tone was completely dispassionate, suggesting it was fine by him if Lyn did. That he was just there to observe.

Lyn shook her head dishonestly.

"She shares your daughter's name," Carlos noted.

"Mmmmhmmm," Lyn replied.

"Why does she?" he asked. "What's the story there?"

Lyn took her time answering, silently remembering the day she'd first found out.

Willa's daughter, Margaret, had called to let Willa know she was a grandmother. Lyn had been washing dishes, content to let the running water drown out the conversation. By the time Willa had hung up the phone and turned toward her, Lyn was drying plates with a freshly laundered towel. She couldn't remember the year or the season, but because she was at Willa's, it must have been a Tuesday or Thursday.

"It's a girl," Willa had said, her voice an odd, strained pitch.

Lyn looked up because of the tone. She wondered whether it meant that something was wrong with the baby, or if perhaps Willa was just being sensitive to the fact that Lyn would never have a grandchild of her own.

"Congratulations," she said evenly.

Willa stood and took a few steps in Lyn's direction. For a moment, Lyn thought she was going to touch her, and she braced herself. But Willa stopped, and rested one small hand on the counter.

"She named her . . ."

Lyn didn't pause her drying. The fact that the baby had been named wasn't earth-shattering news.

"She named her Jiminy," Willa finished.

Lyn didn't drop the towel, but it felt like something inside her was dropping things left and right.

"I don't know why she did, Lyn. I didn't even think she remembered. But she did love Jiminy, and I guess the name stuck in her brain."

Lyn nodded, and kept drying. She set her posture and expression to communicate that she didn't want to talk about it any further. Because Willa didn't either, they'd never discussed it again.

Now, twenty-five years later, this brown-skinned out-of-state investigator was watching her, waiting for her to speak.

"Willa's daughter loved Jiminy," she finally offered. "And remembered her more than we thought she did."

"Your daughter obviously left a deep and lasting impression," Carlos replied. "Even on the mind of a child."

"You have no idea," Lyn replied.

She was frustrated that she couldn't convey just what Jiminy had meant to anyone who came into contact with her. She'd been a miracle, really. She'd always been the most alive, interesting personality in any room. She'd been curious and bold, exceptionally smart and utterly charming. People had fallen for Jiminy whether they'd wanted to or not.

"Did you get along with Willa's daughter, Margaret?" Carlos asked.

"For the first seven years of her life, we did. Then I lost interest."

"After the murders."

"There wasn't much point."

Carlos leaned back in his chair, so that its front two legs rose up in the air. Lyn winced, feeling the strain on the back two legs somewhere deep in her chest.

Carlos noticed and righted himself.

"Edward made them," Lyn explained.

"They're beautiful. I'm sorry, I wasn't thinking."

Lyn nodded. She loved those chairs. She loved running her fingers over them. When she did, she felt almost like she was touching a part of Edward.

"How did Henry and Willa react to the murders?" Carlos asked.

Lyn closed her eyes for a moment. She saw Henry in the room with the doctor and the bodies. Saw him reaching for her, knew she'd stopped him with a stare. He and Willa might've wanted to give her comfort, but she'd moved beyond that by then.

She opened her eyes and stared at the wall.

"They were devastated, same as me," she said. "They didn't go with me to the police station, but they went separately. Equally," she added with a wry half laugh. "They told the sheriff that there had been murders that needed to be prosecuted," she finished, sober once more.

Carlos's face remained still.

"Their report should be somewhere in here," Lyn continued, shuffling the onionskin pile in front of her. "Find that one, too?"

Carlos shook his head.

"Not yet."

Lyn stopped shuffling.

"It's not in this pile?"

Carlos shook his head again. Lyn was silent for a moment.

"I see."

"It doesn't mean it didn't happen," Carlos said. "Back then, people misplaced plenty they didn't want to see the light of day. The sheriff might not've even had a report written in the first place, just to save him the trouble of tearing it up."

"He had one written up of my visit," Lyn said.

"He did," Carlos agreed.

"So."

"You said yourself Willa and Henry were devastated," Carlos said. "I'm sure that they were. Didn't Henry pass away not too long after?"

Lyn nodded. And she didn't say it out loud, but that had probably been for the best.

———

Perched in his lifeguard station at the Fayeville pool, Walton Trawler heard all kinds of things people didn't expect him to. They just forgot about him, sitting up in his chair, keeping his eyes on the water and his fishing hat on his head. They became accustomed to his steady alertness and grew to think of him as an object—as furniture that belonged with the pool, rather than a living, listening human. If they did remember his presence hovering just above them, they thought immediately of his age, and what they assumed was his poor hearing. They didn't consider the possibility that all five of his senses worked as well as a twenty-year-old's, and that he was consequently soaking up every interesting fragment of gossip that floated by. Sound carries over water, even the length of a swimming pool. Walton just sat and listened and learned even more about the town he already knew better than just about anyone. The truth was, his interest in gossip was one of the reasons he kept volunteering for this job, despite his age.

"Was she always trouble?" Gloria Travail was asking, with a flip of her frosted blond hair.

Walton had delivered Gloria twenty-four years ago. He'd taken out her tonsils when she was seven, and her appendix when she was nineteen. The sight of her tanned abdomen always reminded him that he hadn't left a noticeable scar. Gloria flaunted her body for the other people at the pool, most of them women with children. She thrived on contentious relationships and delighted in being a friend one day, a foe the next. She had directed her question at Suze Connors, with whom she'd recently been fighting but had apparently made up. Suze was nursing her new baby under a towel. Walton double-checked to make sure the baby's whole body was covered. He was there to save the lives of anyone who might otherwise drown, but sometimes he just felt like standing up on his chair and yelling at them all to get out of the sun. Wasn't he failing at his duty by watching them slowly kill themselves with cancerous ultraviolet rays? He didn't care as much about himself; he knew his days were numbered.

"I don't know what she was like when she was in Illinois. It's real different there," Suze was saying. "But I never woulda expected something like this. I mean, can you imagine?"

"No, I absolutely cannot," Gloria declared. "The thought of it makes me sick. Where's her momma in all this? What's her grandmomma doing? Though that Willa Hunt is an odd one, I've always thought."

"I expect Willa's just too old and tired and worn out to control her." Suze shook her head sadly. "I told Jiminy to call me up. Told her I'd loveta see her. I wish she'd come to me first."

Gloria patted her arm.

"Don't blame yourself, now. You've had your hands full."

Suze shrugged in a martyrish way and adjusted the towel covering her nursing baby. Her other three kids were playing Marco Polo in the shallow end of the pool, shouting and splashing. The youngest of them was outfitted in water wings that were blown up so tight they looked like they might pop.

"You'd never let one of your kids, would you?" Gloria asked.

"Are you joking?" Suze replied.

She sounded deeply offended.

"I wouldn't, either," Gloria agreed.

"This world's hard enough," Suze said sagely. "Life'll bring you down if you let it, you don't need to bring yourself down ahead of time. I just don't know *what* she was thinking, I honestly don't. He's nice enough, apparently, but that's not the point. He's beneath her."

"For real, sounds like," Gloria said with a snort.

"You're so bad," Suze replied with a shake of her head.

"Maybe this isn't even new for her," Gloria continued. "Maybe he's not her first."

Suze shuddered.

"She should just move along and let Fayeville be."

Gloria opened her dark tanning oil bottle and spread a fresh coat over her browning legs. Suze eyed them enviously. Gloria started giggling.

"What?" Suze asked.

Gloria capped the oil and looked up with a devilish grin.

"Would you rather . . ."

"Oh, Lord, Gloria," Suze rolled her eyes and looked around to make sure her kids were out of earshot.

They were still in the pool, though Bryce was trying to hoist himself up the wrong way onto the waterslide now, followed by Savannah. Melody and her overinflated water wings watched. Suze moved her baby to her other breast.

"Go on," Suze said.

"Would you rather screw a black or a spic?" Gloria asked, her voice low, her wicked smile wide.

The shriek of Walton's whistle pierced the air.

"Not allowed!" he bellowed from the chair above them. "Stop right this second, that is NOT ALLOWED!"

He pretended he was screaming at the kids. Startled, Gloria and Suze covered their ears, and Suze's newborn started wailing.

———

The first thing Bo saw when he pulled up to his aunt Lyn's house was Jiminy sitting on the porch. He hadn't expected her to be there, and he felt unprepared for an encounter. He shifted into reverse to back out before she saw him, but he was too late. She looked up.

He shifted back into drive and continued rolling up to the house, feeling silly for even contemplating flight.

"Hey," he said as he climbed out. "I was surprised to see you here."

"I came with Carlos," Jiminy explained. "He's talking with Lyn."

Bo had yet to meet Carlos, though he appreciated what he and Jiminy were trying to do.

"How's it all going?" he asked.

Jiminy shrugged her pointy shoulders.

"It's going," she said.

She sighed and looked up.

"I don't mean to be like that, it's going well, actually. We're uncovering a lot. I'm just not sure how I fit into it all sometimes."

She couldn't keep the sadness out of her voice, and looking straight into Bo's eyes had been a mistake. She longed to be comforted by him in ways that were no longer possible.

"It seems to me you're the reason it's all happening," Bo replied. "I think that makes you God of the entire operation, which is a pretty good way to fit into anything. Though occasionally thankless, sure. People doubt you, turn their backs on you, take you for granted, take your name in vain. They'll come back to you in the end, though. You just gotta hang in there. Take comfort in your omnipotence."

Jiminy smiled, which made her almost beautiful. Her turned head set her face at a fresh angle, and Bo felt himself falling for her all over again. It wasn't up to him, which was frustrating. It never was.

"Maybe I should come back another time, if they're gonna be a while," Bo said as he turned to leave.

"Are you studying a lot?" Jiminy asked.

"Not enough, probably," he answered. "But I'll pick it up," he continued. "I've just been a little distracted."

"By who?" Jiminy asked sharply.

Bo appreciated the jealousy in her voice and let himself

fantasize briefly about reconciliation, but he knew it wasn't a responsible option. For her sake, he had to be strong.

"No particular who. More of a what. Regular life stuff," he answered. "Listen, I'm gonna head out now and come see Aunt Lyn this evening. I'll catch up with you later on, okay?"

"No!" Jiminy protested.

She hadn't meant to shout. She hadn't meant to say no at all. It had just forced its way out of her, in visceral response to the idea of Bo leaving her again. The power of her objection startled them both.

"Everything all right out here?" came a voice from behind them.

Carlos was in the doorway. Behind him, Lyn looked concerned.

"Everything's fine," Jiminy said, struggling to regain her composure. "Carlos, this is Bo. Bo, please meet Carlos."

"Hey, man," Bo said, reaching out his hand.

"Pleasure," Carlos said, smiling at him.

As the two men shook, Lyn moved out onto the porch.

"Anything wrong?" Lyn asked her great-nephew.

She hadn't been expecting Bo in the middle of the afternoon. She worried something unpleasant had driven him to seek her out when he otherwise would have been studying under the hickory tree, divining the secrets of the mass of blood and muscle and tissue we humans dragged around day after day after day.

"Everything's fine," Bo reassured her. "I didn't mean to interrupt, didn't know you had company. Just wanted to check in."

Lyn looked from him to Jiminy. She saw the flush in the girl's cheeks and the agitation in both their postures. She sighed.

"There's absolutely no reason you two can't be friends," she said.

Jiminy and Bo looked quickly at Lyn, surprised.

"We know that, Aunt Lyn," Bo said.

"And we are," Jiminy chimed in. "We will be."

"No reason," Lyn repeated. "No reason at all . . ."

She trailed off, suddenly feeling completely worn out. She knew they were all staring at her as she sank down to take a seat on the porch steps, but she kept her head bowed. Gravity had gotten the best of her for the day—she was ready to concede defeat.

From her new vantage point, she could see a village of ants stretching themselves thin from their hill toward unknown destinations through the grass and into the woods. She wondered if they ever slept as she watched a group of them carry a dead cricket on their backs. Such strength! Such endurance! She marveled at their ability to march steadily on, underneath such an outsized burden, myopically undeterred.

––––––––

Later, at the Comfort Inn, Carlos flipped through the channels of his small, unsatisfactory television. He didn't care what he watched; he was in search of the numbness that comes with staring at a screen in an artificially dark room on a sunny day. He needed to give his brain a rest.

He settled on a national newscast, which was breathlessly covering the story of a missing eighteen-year-old from a suburb of Minneapolis. Apparently, the girl had made a cell phone call to her boyfriend from the parking lot of a mall and mentioned that she was scared someone was following her. Her phone had turned up two days later in a Dumpster four miles away, but there still hadn't been any trace of her. The newscaster gave an update on the hundreds of volunteers conducting all-night searches and urged anyone with information to please call. He showed a full-screen photo of the missing young woman, who had curly blond hair and a cherubic face, complete with dimples. She was adorable, and, Carlos guessed, also dead.

He sighed and turned the TV off. When Carlos was on the road, he didn't let himself think too much about home, but at the moment, he was missing it. He closed his eyes briefly and let himself imagine he was back there. Not where he lived now, but where he had grown up, in a house in the woods by a creek.

This was the place he mentally went to relax. He'd never taken a meditation class, but he was familiar with the essential "go to your happy place" concept. Carlos didn't consider himself a well-adjusted person generally. He was haunted and driven, with little time for comfort-seeking. But he understood the value of a calm, clear mind, and over the years, he'd developed his own mode of achieving it.

The creek had been his constant companion as a youth. His bedroom window had opened up to it, so he'd read and dressed and slept to the sound of rushing water all his growing-up years. He'd ridden a raft down it, caught crawdads in it, and studied all the various plants and trees beside it. Along its banks, he'd become fascinated with sweet gum, tupelo, bald cypress, Spanish moss, prickly pear cactus, and all different species of pine. When the rain came, the creek would swell and spill, threatening to swamp the little house his family owned. Carlos had always been aware of the potential damage, and he was sensitive to his parents' stress, but he couldn't help but side with the creek. If it wanted to go for more, he was with it all the way.

In his mental visitations to this childhood sanctuary, Carlos would stretch himself out in the moss on the sunny side of the creek, with one leg dipped in the water and the rest of him comfortably sprawled. His eyes would be closed, his ears open, his mouth and nose filled with freshness. He could practically feel the cold water ebbing around his shin, and he imagined it seeping into him, traveling up through his body and into his head to cool his overheated brain.

He held this sensation as he consciously turned his cooled mind toward his current case. There was something that was bothering him about it; some sense that Lyn knew more than she'd revealed. He wondered if he'd be able to coax it from her, or hit upon it some other way. This is what he turned his mind to. Experience had taught Carlos a few things, and he knew that at the intersection of relaxation and concentration lay some of his most important breakthroughs. He headed there now, with his eyes still closed, purposely wading deeper into the waters.

Down the road at Tortillas, Rosa had been nervous about the man staying at the Comfort Inn. She'd spotted him the day before and hadn't had time to investigate who he might be, so she was left agitated by paranoid assumptions.

Ever since the incident with the chairs and the trucks full of brutal young men, Rosa had been fearful of further trouble. She worried that someone had put in a call to Immigration and that deportation was imminent.

She'd heard that the government had begun employing professional Latino men for immigration assignments, and she was now convinced that this explained the stranger's presence. He might look like her and speak her language, but he could be her worst enemy, sneaking up.

Juan was in the United States legally, but Rosa was not. Even being the mother of an American citizen couldn't change her status. Opening their restaurant had been a risk, but they'd put Juan's name on everything and hoped that positively contributing to the life of this small Mississippi town would grant them some amount of karmic amnesty. It felt more constructive and proactive than lying low and barely scraping by.

Still, Rosa was periodically terrorized by the idea that she might be forcibly separated from her husband and daughter. If she was found out and deported, she wasn't sure what they would do. They'd left Mexico for a fresh start and a better life, and she hated thinking she could be the reason they'd have to give it all up. But she also couldn't stand the notion of being separated from Juan and Penelope. Would she insist that they stay on without her? And if she did, would Juan agree to this arrangement? The possibility that he would made her prematurely angry with him. She recognized that this was a regrettable consequence of her paranoia, and a self-sabotaging one. Because the more short-tempered and unreasonably bitter she acted now, the more likely her husband would opt for the enforced separation rather than returning with her to a place they'd decided they didn't want to be. Unfortunately, the more she contemplated this likelihood, the more angry and bitter she became. And her bad mood was only worsened by her realization that if these were their last days together without her knowing it, she was wasting them on acrimony. Rosa had worked herself into an emotional sand trap.

To make matters worse, the baby had become increasingly colicky, keeping them up all night, almost every night. Rosa had tried everything she could think of, but nothing seemed to work. If something was really wrong, she wasn't sure what they were going to do. Rosa was wracked with worry, dangerously sleep-deprived, and generally all-around miserable.

When she had first come to Fayeville three years previous, people had been so much friendlier. They hadn't bent over backwards to make her feel welcome, but neither had they gone out of their way to try to make her leave. But attitudes had changed in the last few years. More and more of her fellow countryfolk had arrived, so perhaps the town had just reached some invisible tolerance threshold. Whatever the explanation, something basic had gone sour.

She tried to focus on her empanadas to give herself a break from her wretchedness. Empanadas were something she could handle. They took time and effort—particularly the secret-recipe, melt-in-your-mouth empanadas for which she was legendary—but she knew she could turn them out perfectly. As long as she had the ingredients and a working oven, she could coax the desired results. In Mexico, in Mississippi, at various roadside kitchens in between, Rosa had whipped up her empanadas in a variety of circumstances. And the results were always the same. People called her gifted, indispensable, a wizard. They considered themselves lucky to have been able to taste her masterpiece just once. This made her happy, it was true. But Rosa would give it all up in a moment if she could instead find as reliable a recipe for how to keep her family safe and whole.

When the bell on the front door jangled, Rosa peeked out between the slats of the screen that separated the kitchen from the main room, then gasped quietly and backed away.

It was the government immigration officer. He was coming for her after all.

"Anyone here?" he called.

Rosa weighed her options. She could scoot out the back door, but then the man would have the run of the place, and her empanadas would burn. Plus, she'd be giving him reason to suspect her. Better to act normal, charming, American.

"Be right with you!" she called back.

She held up a scrubbed pan to check her reflection, then smoothed her hair back and pinched her cheeks. She patted down her shirt and skirt, took a deep breath, and walked into the main room.

The man and his companion were still standing by the door, not fully committing to the inside space.

"You open for business?" the man asked.

Rosa smiled accommodatingly.

"Sure, what can I get for you?"

"*Que nos recomienda?*" he asked.

She hesitated for only a moment, then smiled.

"What do I recommend?" she replied in English.

She looked at the man until he nodded, determined to show that she needed to check the accuracy of her Spanish comprehension.

"It's all delicious," she said. "I have empanadas fresh from the oven."

"Perfect. And how about a Corona?"

Rosa had beer back in the fridge for her and Juan, but she wasn't legally allowed to sell it until Tortillas was granted its liquor license, which might never happen given the county's reluctance to "encourage debauchery," as it had been put in a recent Fayeville City Council meeting.

"If I gave you one, it would have to be our secret," she replied.

He looked confused, but the young woman with him smiled.

"Fayeville was a dry county till recently," she explained to him. "Lots of places still can't serve alcohol."

Rosa nodded. She'd made it clear that she was willing to provide though, partially because she wanted to gauge the man's openness to bending rules. She knew that she was risking the possibility that this was another test and that she should adhere as closely to the law as possible to deny him any reason to find fault, but she was beginning to hope that he wasn't there to bust her after all. She was gambling on his developing an affinity for her.

"I'll keep it between us, I promise," the man said to Rosa.

She smiled.

"I'll take one, too," the young woman added.

Juan found Rosa at the refrigerator, retrieving the Coronas from the crisper drawer where they kept them cold.

"What's going on?" he asked.

She looked up at his still-swollen lip and resisted the urge to press the chilled bottle in her hand against it. This was for their guests, who needed to like them. Whether or not the man was with Immigration, it had now become important to Rosa to win him over. It gave her a mission besides being scared and resentful. It was a way back, after the thugs in the pickup trucks had thrown her off track.

"Late night customers. I'm giving them empanadas and beer. Is Pen sleeping?"

Juan shook his head, noting for the umpteenth time the irony of the fact that the Hispanic pronunciation of their colicky baby's nickname made it a homonym of "pain."

"Not yet, but she's quiet. She's staring at the mobile, and my cousin's listening for her."

Juan's cousin worked in the hospital, and she'd provided Rosa with the leftover magazines that she'd used to make the mobile. Rosa had cut out the perfume ads and attached them to a resculpted wire hanger. She liked the ones with people she recognized, that had scented strips included, so she'd searched especially for those. Now her baby could stare up at various floating celebrities, all smelling like flowers.

Rosa filled a basket with tortilla chips and poured some salsa into a bowl.

"Here, let me help," Juan offered.

He gathered some water glasses and a bottle of his hot sauce and followed his wife into the main room. He'd noticed that she seemed alive again, and he didn't want to miss a moment of it.

Jiminy had knocked on Carlos's motel room door two hours before, waking him from the nap he'd accidentally slipped into during his meditative efforts. Carlos had been surprised to see her.

"Hi," he said, as he tried to remember whether they'd been scheduled to meet.

They hadn't. Not till the next day, when they were going to interview the former sheriff together. Jiminy was clutching something in her arms. From the way she looked at him, Carlos was aware that he represented something important to her. Some brand of salvation, it seemed. He knew this was dangerous. He moved to allow her to come inside.

"I hope I'm not bothering you," she said.

"You're not. What time is it?" he asked, gripping the wrist where he normally wore his watch.

He could see it lying on the bedside table. When had he taken it off? Had he been planning to sleep after all? It was dark out now, and it had been midday when he'd lain down.

Jiminy checked the watch strapped to one of her thin little wrists. To Carlos, everything about her seemed problematically delicate.

"Nine thirty," she answered.

"Wow," Carlos replied, running his hands through his hair.

"At night," she added.

Carlos grinned.

"You can tell I'm a bit turned around. What brings you here?"

"I wanted to show you this," she replied, indicating the album she still had clutched to her chest. "My grandmother gave it to me."

Actually, it had been waiting for Jiminy on her bed with a note from Willa, who had apparently gone out. Willa preferred to communicate in absentia whenever possible.

The note read, "Your grandfather's photos. Use them if they can help. The litter box needs changing."

The last line had been added in a different colored pen, most likely after Willa had entered Jiminy's room and discovered the kitten she'd been secretly keeping. Cholera had still been there when Jiminy came in, so at least Willa hadn't opted for an immediate removal. Jiminy waited for her grandmother to return, since they obviously had much to discuss, but as it grew later, she grew increasingly restless. Especially after looking at the pictures, Jiminy didn't want to be alone. She tried calling Bo, but he wasn't home, and she then spent too long torturing herself with thoughts of what he might be doing. Finally, she started walking. Along the way, she forced herself to turn toward the motel where Carlos was staying, away from the road that led to Bo's trailer.

And so she'd woken Carlos, who was now gazing down at her chest. In his defense, that's where the album still rested.

"I'm really hungry," Jiminy said, suddenly realizing she was.

Behind her, lights flickered in the restaurant down the road. Carlos glanced toward it, then back down at the young woman beside him. He liked the way she smelled.

"Well, let's get you taken care of then," he replied. "You up for some Mexican?"

He hadn't meant it at all the way someone else might take it. But he'd said it; it was out there. Jiminy smiled, and he searched her smile for slyness.

"You bet," she answered, before he could be sure of anything.

A short time later they were sitting across from each other at a bright blue table, having just finished their second beer each, along with a delicious meal. Carlos looked at Jiminy expectantly.

"Here," she said, pushing the album across the table toward him.

Carlos looked carefully at each photo. The one of Willa made her seem accessible enough, though fuzzy and slightly out of focus. Lyn was unmistakable. A younger olive tree, smokier and smoother.

When Carlos reached the group of photos in the envelope at the back, he breathed in sharply.

"I know," Jiminy said.

"Who took these?" Carlos asked.

"My grandfather," Jiminy answered. "He was a carpenter who couldn't work with wood and a photographer who never told anyone."

"He was a journalist," Carlos replied. "These aren't candids. These are for a record."

Jiminy scooted her chair around the table so she could be next to Carlos and see the pictures with him.

"They were all so young," she said pointlessly.

Carlos looked down at the back of her bent head, watching how her dark hair fell like a river down her neck. He breathed in her tropical scent.

"Do you think Henry knew who killed Edward and Jiminy?" Jiminy raised her head to ask. "Do you think anyone does?"

Carlos nodded.

"Yes, I imagine some people do."

"How do we find them? How do we get them to talk?" she asked.

Carlos gazed at her.

"We work," he replied. "And we think, and we plan. We hope for some lucky breaks. And if we get them, I call the FBI and they open a federal case alleging civil rights violations. We compel people to testify under oath. But to get to that point, we've got a lot of work to do. Can you handle it?"

Jiminy nodded.

"Now that I'm a law school dropout, I've got all the time in the world," she replied.

Carlos took another sip of his beer.

"Why'd you quit?" he asked.

"Too much work," Jiminy said wryly. "Or at least too much pointless work that didn't seem to really help anyone. So I bailed, and came here, and stumbled across this awful thing that happened, and now all I want is to find out who did it and get justice, which is why I need someone who knows the law," she finished sardonically.

"So maybe you'll reconsider?" Carlos asked. "Take it up again?"

Jiminy shook her head.

"I'm not cut out to be a lawyer. I don't know what I'm cut out for. I wish I wasn't such a coward."

"A coward?" Carlos repeated.

Jiminy nodded. "Through and through."

Carlos shook his head.

"I've met plenty of cowards," he said. "Trust me, you're not one."

"Oh, give me a little time," Jiminy answered. "Anyway, I don't think I ever really wanted to be a lawyer."

"What did you want to be?"

She took a moment to consider.

"Brave," she finally answered. "Someone who makes an impact. But considering I can't even make it through law school . . ."

"Why'd you come here?"

"Random impulse. First place that popped into my head. Possibly because I saw a T-shirt that said 'Tupelo Honey.' "

"And then you just happened to uncover this long-buried crime and decided to try to solve it."

"Yeah."

Carlos looked at her steadily.

"Sounds pretty brave and impactful to me."

Jiminy thought about this. She smiled.

"We'll see."

She took another sip of her beer and noticed that the bottle was almost empty.

"It must be past midnight," she remarked.

Rosa emerged from the kitchen, where she'd been watching through the screen slats.

"More Corona?" she asked.

"I think just the bill," Carlos replied.

Rosa placed it on the table.

"To the chef of the greatest empanadas I've ever tasted," Carlos said, lifting his bottle to Rosa.

"Here, here," Jiminy agreed.

Rosa smiled, reassured from her spying that she had nothing to fear. Though she wasn't positive what these two meant to each other, she was grateful that they meant her no harm. The rest really wasn't any of her business.

Outside, the night sky was clear. Jiminy threw her arms straight up in a "V" as she dropped her head back to take in the stars. Carlos could tell she was a little tipsy. She twirled once and grabbed his arm to steady herself.

"Whoops, sorry," she laughed.

Her hand was warm against his skin.

"I better head home," she declared, so sweet and straightforward.

He caught her arm before she could move away.

"You don't have to," he said. "Why don't you stay?"

Through her beer haze, Jiminy was surprised. She hadn't thought of Carlos as a romantic prospect. She hadn't thought of anyone besides Bo, with whom she was still completely preoccupied. She was certainly in awe of Carlos, and she longed to be respected and appreciated by him, but she hadn't explored how being appreciated by him would manifest itself. She hadn't envisioned anything physical beyond a pat on the head or a chaste kiss on the cheek that would be more high-five than high passion. She'd half-pictured Carlos lifting her up by her waist and swinging her around. None of these images warranted more than a G rating from the Imagination Picture Association.

But now here they were, and he was moving closer in order to . . . what? Kiss like actual adults? She wasn't sure she wanted that, though she couldn't help but feel excited.

Before she had sorted out exactly how to handle the situation, they were startled by the screech of sirens.

———

Bo had been to Fayeville Hospital a handful of times for broken bones and visits to ailing relatives, but this was his first time on the premises since he'd begun his medical training. When he envisioned himself as a doctor, he pictured working someplace far from Fayeville, but he did harbor a secret fantasy of being begged to return to perform a complicated operation for which someone needed the very best pediatric surgeon around. He imagined getting the call and magnanimously deciding to return to a town that had never made him feel welcome or valued. He'd show up, perform a medical miracle, and then leave again, leaving them in awe of his mind-boggling talent. Bo turned this fantasy over in his brain again as he crossed the parking lot and opened the door into the small waiting room that was filled with people he knew.

He saw Jiminy first, which didn't surprise him. His eyes were trained to seek her out, it seemed. And after all, she was the one who'd called and asked him to come.

She looked like she'd been there all night, which now that he thought about it, she probably had. She was wearing a man's button-down shirt over a sundress and flip-flops, and her long dark hair was gathered in a messy bun speared by a pencil.

Nearby sat Jean Butrell and Walton Trawler, bent over a book of crosswords. Jean's eyes were red and puffy, and Walton looked exhausted with the strain of distracting and comforting her. Bo had heard that they were a couple, but this was the first evidence he'd seen of it.

Sitting across from them, alone, was his great-aunt Lyn, who'd come with the list of Willa's medicines. She seemed elsewhere when Bo looked into her eyes. Mentally vacant. Bo wondered where she'd gone.

"How is she?" Bo asked the room.

Jiminy looked up.

"Not stable yet," she said. "She's crashed three times and they said we still might lose her."

Jean let out a tiny wail.

"I'm so sorry," Bo said. "Heart attack?"

"And a stroke," Jiminy nodded. "Thank God she had time to call Jean before it got too bad."

"Not the kind of call you expect at midnight," Jean sobbed. "I could barely hear her, her voice was so weak."

"You weren't home with her?" Bo asked.

Jiminy shook her head, looking down at the floor, thinking of all the germs and pain that had been spilled there.

The doors opened behind Bo, and Carlos walked in with a tray of coffees and a bag of donuts from the new café at Hush-Mart.

"I've got an extra coffee if you want it," Carlos said to Bo as he passed the cups around and took the seat next to Jiminy.

"No, thanks, I'm all set," Bo said slowly, looking from Carlos's white undershirt to the oversized button-down Jiminy was wearing.

Jiminy wouldn't meet his gaze. She was still staring at the floor, and her cheeks were burning. Nothing had actually happened with Carlos, but Jiminy still felt guilty, and this confused her.

"Come sit here," Lyn said suddenly.

Everyone else turned because it was the first thing she'd said in hours. Lyn was looking at Bo, stretching her arm out toward him.

"Come sit next to me."

"I'll be right there," Bo replied, before turning back to Jiminy.

"Was there something you needed?" he asked her.

He'd assumed when she called him that she needed something from him specifically, but perhaps she'd found it elsewhere. He hadn't expected her to move on so quickly.

"I was worried about Lyn," Jiminy said softly. "We're all upset, but she seemed to just switch herself off and go blank."

Bo nodded. Jiminy finally looked at him and he could see anguish in her eyes. He turned away and walked to the other side of the room, where he sunk into a chair next to his great-aunt, feeling more related to her than ever before; neither of them could be comforted.

Jiminy resumed staring at the ground. She longed to be next to Bo. If it were up to her, she'd still be with him, but it wasn't. He'd ended their relationship, and she'd been forced to accept that. As unhappy as she was about it.

"Did you hear back from your mom?" Carlos asked.

She shook her head.

"I left word with the cruise ship company. And gave them the emergency room number to pass along to her."

"I haven't done anything about the interviews we had set up for today," Carlos said quietly. "But I can postpone them till tomorrow. Or even later."

"No, you go," Jiminy answered. "Too much time has been wasted already, and we don't know how much we've got left."

Her grandmother had reminded them of that. As the clock ticked on, who knew who else they might lose?

Carlos nodded.

"I'll come back when they're through," he said, placing a steady hand on Jiminy's shoulder.

"You want your shirt back?" she asked.

Carlos shook his head.

"You'll be cold in this AC, you keep it."

Carlos squeezed her shoulder, offering a snatch of added warmth, then pulled away. Out of the corner of his eye, Bo watched him leave.

A Latina in orderly scrubs pushed through the doors that separated the waiting room from the rest of Fayeville Hospital, and Jiminy sat up straighter, expecting an update. But the woman avoided eye contact as she set about rearranging the magazines and picking up trash from the floor. Jiminy slumped back into her chair, despondent once more.

Across from her, Jean had gotten a new round of quiet sobs under control. She stood up, gripped her loose tunic at its hem, and tugged downward to smooth it over her slacks. The motion seemed to give her confidence, which she used for forward momentum.

"I just need to use the ladies' room," Jean said to Walton, and whoever else might be listening.

Near Jiminy's chair, she stumbled and nearly fell. Jiminy leapt up and caught her shoulder. Jean was embarrassed.

"I don't do well without sleep," she explained. "I'm feeling so drained."

"Let me help you," Jiminy replied.

Jean leaned against her, and the two of them made their way to the restroom door.

Inside, Jiminy heard Jean sobbing in her stall and worked to hold back her own tears. She felt raw and fragile, worried ragged.

The toilet flushed and Jean emerged, red-eyed and sniffling.

"This is just too much for her, you know," she said.

There was accusation in her voice. Jiminy braced herself.

"She told me on the phone," Jean continued. "She could barely speak, but she said to me, 'I'm not strong enough for this. I'm just too tired now. I don't want to disappoint her, but I'm just too tired.'"

Jiminy stayed quiet, watching Jean's trembling lips.

"She couldn't take the stress of what you're bringing down on us. Maybe if it was five or ten years ago, maybe then. But she's exhausted now, and you're forcing her to relive the worst experience of her life. You're forcing all of us to do that. Why? Is it really worth it?"

Jean flung these questions through the air like so many quivering daggers. Before Jiminy could address them, or raise her shield, there was a knock on the door.

"The nurse wants to see you," Walton called.

It felt strange to Walton to be back in the hospital he'd presided over for fifty-plus years. He was surprised at how many young people were now in positions of authority. He'd begun when he was in his twenties, but now that he was aware of how little he'd really known during those years, he was alarmed that the world was still letting youngsters take it over. It made everything feel very unstable. It made him feel unsafe.

Sitting in the waiting room comforting Jean was not where Walton wanted to be. He'd have prefered to be in the operating room, with his medical coat and surgical tools, making life-or-death decisions. His strongest memories of the waiting room were all about telling people bad news. He'd also given people good news here, but good news in an emergency room was relative. It was good news that your loved one was going to live, but more than likely, just a short while before, it hadn't crossed your mind that there was any alternative. This room was about sudden accidents and bad luck. Walton didn't care to linger here.

Remembering his doctoring days did afford him a uniquely clinical frame of mind, which came in handy amid all the emotions running wild. He felt he could analyze the situation better than his companions, and he put this talent to use as he checked in on how they were all faring.

He found it a little peculiar that Lyn was still waiting. He wondered if it was out of a sense of obligation, or paralyzing concern, or simply inertia. She'd spent most of her life waiting on Willa in some form or another. Perhaps she couldn't see her way out of the pattern.

He didn't question that she was genuinely worried. He understood there was real affection between Willa and Lyn, and he knew Lyn's life would be seriously impacted should Willa pass on. But Walton wondered whether it wouldn't also be a release of some sort. He wondered whether or not Lyn was quietly struggling to keep from acknowledging a dark wish for the worst, as she sat silent and frozen in her corner of the room, where she was still gripping her great-nephew's arm.

The young man really did look uncannily like Edward. He was lighter skinned, but otherwise a spitting image. Supposedly, he was studying to be a doctor.

Walton hadn't recognized the nurse who strode through the doorway, but he'd recognized the look of purpose on her face. She'd come to tell them something. Walton had crossed to the bathroom door and knocked.

————

As Jiminy was led to see her grandmother, she glanced sidelong at the doctor whom Walton had mistaken for a nurse. She was only a few years older than Jiminy, but she appeared considerably more weathered and drawn. And more accomplished, clearly. Her name tag read "Dr. Connors," which made Jiminy wonder if she was any relation to Suze. Everyone in Fayeville tended to be related one way or another. The doctor opened the door to Willa's room.

"We need to monitor your grandmother very closely for the next forty-eight hours. She's sedated, so she probably won't wake up, but you can talk to her. She can hear you."

Visitors liked being told that patients could hear them, even when this wasn't necessarily true. The doctor had no problem comforting people with harmless fiction. So often, she had to hurt them with unavoidable, cruel facts.

Jiminy nodded and crossed the cramped room to the bed, breathing carefully to control the panic she felt at seeing tubes snaking in and out of her grandmother's body. The doctor lingered for a moment to check Willa's heartbeat before leaving grandmother and granddaughter alone.

"Hi," Jiminy said softly, taking Willa's hand in her own.

They both had small hands. Willa's felt thin and papery, like a breeze might blow it away. It reminded Jiminy of the onion-skin transcript Carlos had found. She traced the lines of her grandmother's palm with her finger, trying to remember what they represented. One was her lifeline, she knew. The other was for love. And the number of children could be divined, or so people claimed. All of Willa's lines were short, deep creases. Jiminy covered them with her palm.

"How are you feeling?" she asked, keeping her voice soft and hopefully soothing. "I know we haven't been particularly close, but I love you. And I'm sorry if I did this to you. I didn't mean to. I really didn't."

Jiminy bowed her head and let her tears have their way.

————————

Half an hour later, Willa fluttered her fingers. Jiminy looked up, startled.

Willa's eyes were closed, her lips parted. She had oxygen tubes inserted in her nostrils to help her breathe, but Jiminy saw that she was inhaling and exhaling through her mouth, reclaiming her life on her own terms.

"It's not your fault," Willa said.

Jiminy felt relieved and humbled. In Willa's state, fighting to come back, she was still attempting to comfort another.

"You were doing it for Jiminy, I know."

It was a quick trip from relieved and humbled to confused and concerned.

"I'm Jiminy, Grandma," Jiminy said.

Willa kept her eyes closed but squeezed her hand.

"No, no, dear, Jiminy died. I'm sorry. You were so young, you didn't understand. I know you loved her. There was so much you couldn't understand."

Before Jiminy could argue or investigate further, the doctor entered the room.

"She woke up?" she asked.

"I don't know," Jiminy replied. "Sort of. She hasn't opened her eyes but she's talking and moving a little."

The doctor examined Willa and checked the machines to which she was hooked.

"Miz Hunt?" she said loudly and clearly. "Miz Hunt, can you hear me?"

Willa didn't stir. She again appeared to be sleeping.

"She wasn't making any sense," Jiminy replied. "I think she may have thought I was my mother."

The doctor frowned.

"She had multiple strokes. We won't know the full damage till I do some more tests. Even if she comes out of this completely fine, it would be very normal to have disorientation after a trauma like this. It happens in people a fraction of her age, so I would certainly expect it to happen to her. Excuse me a moment."

The doctor glanced down at her pager then back up.

"If she moves or speaks again, will you press that button?" she asked Jiminy, as she hurried from the room.

That was something Jiminy felt sure she could do. Pushing people's buttons had become a specialty.

When Roy Tomlins pulled into the driveway of Brayer Plantation, he was surprised by the activity on the sprawling front lawn. Travis Brayer's son Bobby, the state senator and candidate for governor, formed the epicenter of a mini-tornado of action. Roy saw cameras, cords, boom microphones, sunglasses, clipboards, water bottles, and large shiny discs that a man and a woman were angling and adjusting in different directions. Bobby appeared unfazed by it all, cool as usual in blue jeans and a button-down shirt tucked snug by a large American flag belt buckle. He was talking into the camera, until the noise from Roy's truck proved too distracting.

"Cut!" a man with a bullhorn exclaimed with exasperation. "Who is this? What's going on?"

He was glaring at his crew, who were all shaking their heads that they didn't know. Whoever had failed to stop this intruder at the gate and instruct him to wait for the all-clear sign between takes was clearly in trouble.

If the director had targeted his accusatory questions toward Travis's perch on the veranda, Travis would've been happy to tell him that the truck belonged to his friend Roy, who was coming to visit him at exactly the time Travis had instructed, smack in the middle of the shoot.

Travis was pleased to watch the cloud of dust from Roy's truck descend on the group surrounding his son. It was the first break in a bad mood that had been worsening ever since he'd been rolled out onto the veranda earlier that morning.

"How ya doin', Dad?" Bobby had called back then, in his booming, good-natured, people-are-observing-me voice.

Travis had nodded at him, wishing he didn't have a blanket on his lap. Only the old or infirm needed blankets on warm days. Travis knew he was both, but he preferred not to dress the part if he could help it. The nurse had put the blanket there, and he'd forgotten. But of course then all the people on the lawn had turned to look at him, and he had recognized the indulgent condescension in their eyes. It was the same look his wife had given the mentally challenged bird feeder salesman that used to come around—so encouraging of someone from whom she expected so little. To these people, Travis was sweetly pathetic. Their simpering smiles disgusted him.

"He's adorable," the makeup lady had exclaimed.

Travis had heard this distinctly. His ears were two of the only body parts that had yet to betray him.

So Travis was now pleased to have these people's work disrupted by Roy's arrival. Roy continued driving straight up to him, aware that the dust and noise made by his truck were sending the bullhorn blowhard into paroxysms. He even drove a little faster than he needed to and gave a couple honks for good measure. The chairs in the back of his truck were strapped down tight enough, and the smile on Travis's face made it all worth it.

"Mornin', Trav," Roy called as he climbed out of his truck.

"Morning, Roy. You got the chairs?"

"You bet."

Roy was thrilled to be there. He and Travis had been friends for seventy years, but they'd never been equals. Roy was more sycophant than confidant, which suited Travis just fine. He valued deference in his companions.

Travis could see his son striding across the lawn. This walk wasn't for the cameras, which were being reset for another take. Bobby was headed for them.

"Mr. Tomlins, I thought that was you," he said to Roy as he took the porch steps two at a time.

He was taller than Travis by several inches, and he'd inherited his mother's untapped athleticism. He moved well, Travis admitted, aware that he should take some pride in this.

"Well, hi there, Bobby," Roy said, shaking hands with Travis's son. "You sure got yourself into something these days."

Bobby laughed deeply and turned to a short man with curly brown hair and glasses who'd been trailing him.

"David, I'd like you to meet one of my dad's oldest friends, someone who's known me since I was a baby," Bobby said to the curly-haired man.

"Since before you were a baby," Roy said.

Bobby laughed again.

"Since even before," he agreed. "David Eisen, meet Mr. Roy Tomlins. Mr. Tomlins, meet David Eisen. David's a writer for *Esquire* magazine, doin' a profile on up-and-comin' Southern leaders."

In truth, Bobby had been apprehensive about letting any journalist too close to his father or his father's friends, but his press secretary had convinced him that they'd get a much better story if they allowed a more intimate level of access. Bobby prayed she was right, and decided to mask his worry with aggressive good cheer, willing everything to go well with the sheer force of his winning demeanor.

In the glow of Bobby's thousand-watt smile, Roy looked David Eisen over before shaking his hand. He didn't particularly want to shake it, but he realized it was the thing to do. He noticed that the writer was holding something small and gray that he brought close to Roy's mouth when Roy started to speak, which made him step back.

"It's just a digital recorder," the writer explained.

"Oh," Roy said, hesitatingly stepping forward again.

He didn't know whether to direct his comments to the writer or the machine. He was supremely uncomfortable.

"Well, Bobby's a leader all right," he managed. "Always has been."

Bobby beamed and clapped Roy lightly on his shoulder as
David Eisen looked Roy straight in the eyes. The sunlight reflecting off the writer's glasses was blinding. Roy blinked in
irritation.

"What do you have there?" David asked, pointing to the
back of Roy's truck.

It was Travis who answered, grinning all the while.

"Some stolen property he recovered for me. Let's get a look,
Roy."

Roy walked to the back of his truck and struggled to put his
foot on the bumper. He felt like his body was growing stiffer
and creakier by the day. Still, at least he wasn't wheelchair-bound
like Travis yet.

"Here, let me help ya," Bobby boomed. "Wanna get a little
dirty, David?"

David did not.

He stayed put while Bobby launched himself into the bed of
Roy's truck and began undoing the straps.

"These are some purty chairs, Mr. Tomlins. Dad, you said
they belonged to you?"

Travis nodded.

"Had 'em made special," he replied. "Haven't seen 'em in
thirty some years."

Bobby hoisted one of the chairs over his head unnecessarily
and jumped to the ground with it, then placed it in front of his
father.

"They look good as new," he said.

Roy watched the *Esquire* writer run his fingers over the
wood and resisted the urge to slap his hand away.

"K.S.O.," David Eisen read. "Is that someone's initials?"

Roy saw a look of surprised alarm cross Bobby's face. Saw

him check the label himself and turn back toward the commercial shoot, ready to lead David Eisen away.

"It's just an old name," Bobby answered. "You know what? I'd like nothin' better than to keep sittin' here and jawin', but I think we gotta take advantage of this weather and finish up. Know what they say: 'Make hay while the sun shines!'"

He grinned as he placed his big hand on the writer's shoulder.

"Well, it was nice to meet you, Mr. Tomlins," David Eisen said. "And these *are* beautiful chairs, Mr. Brayer. You say they were stolen from you?"

"That's right," Travis replied. "By some good-for-nothin' spics."

David Eisen looked up quickly.

"Dad, you don't mean that," Bobby said sharply.

There was panic and reprimand in his voice. Roy looked from son to father and back again. Travis seemed completely calm, which made Roy love him all the more. He already had quite a story to tell the boys. He was recording it in his memory for later, just as carefully as David Eisen was recording it on his little machine.

"He doesn't mean that," Bobby said to the writer.

"What *do* you mean, exactly?" David asked Travis in a quiet, curious voice.

Travis waved a hand in front of his face.

"I don't mean that all wetbacks are good for nothin'," Travis clarified. "I just mean the ones that sneak in here to steal jobs and such, which is most of 'em. They take whatever they can get their dirty hands on. They're just as bad as the nig—"

"That's enough, Dad," Bobby interrupted sharply.

Roy had never heard Bobby speak that way to his father, though he'd also never heard Travis speak quite the way he was speaking either, at least not in this sort of company. Travis was usually quite careful around Bobby and his political friends. He wasn't an old man unaware that the times had changed. He knew exactly what sort of impact he was capable of having by saying such things in front of such people.

"He's not well," Bobby said to David Eisen. "He's had some serious health problems that have damaged his body and brain. I hope you'll respect that fact and keep all this off the record. Out of decency. He's just a fragile, dying old man who doesn't know what he's saying."

"Don't talk to me like that, boy!" Travis bellowed.

He stood up from his wheelchair, which was something that had been deemed medically impossible in his condition. To Roy, it didn't seem that Travis's legs were supporting him at all. He appeared to be empowered by a pure, undiluted rage. His face was flushed purple, and outsized veins in his neck were throbbing as he pointed a crooked finger at his son.

"You respect me, understand? You show me some respect!"

Before any of the others could reach for him, Travis Brayer toppled hard onto his side and slid headfirst down the veranda stairs to the gravel driveway below. He gave a groan as his head hit and the rest of his body piled after, like a Slinky made of worn-out old man.

———

Lyn knew people who crossed themselves or folded their hands in prayer whenever they heard the sound of ambulance sirens. For most of her adult life, she'd felt resentful toward them for doing this. The fact that whoever was injured was being rushed to the hospital and tended to seemed like prize enough. The prayers were just rubbing in how privileged they were. No sirens had raced to her husband and daughter, and no strangers had prayed for them, as far as she knew. To her, ambulance sirens were an elusive luxury.

Even when her daughter, Jiminy, had split her leg open on a tractor blade, no one besides Lyn, Edward, and Henry had rushed to care for her. The receptionist at Fayeville Hospital had claimed they didn't have the time to treat her, and recommended they give the veterinarian's office a try instead. Henry had stormed past the desk and made a direct appeal to the doctor, who'd agreed to stitch Jiminy up. Lyn looked across at that doctor now, sitting with Jean, both of them dozing off. She'd heard others claim that Walton Trawler was a decent man now, but he certainly hadn't started out that way. In her experience, very few had.

By the time the sirens had pulled to a stop outside the Fayeville Hospital door, Lyn could tell that they were louder than normal. The crescendo sounded as though it was being caused by a whole fleet of ambulances. Before she could stand to look out the window, assuming she had any inclination to investigate what emergencies others might be facing, the doors opened and a crowd poured in. She saw state troopers and cameramen and Roy Tomlins. And an ambulance gurney that was whisked past, shielded by EMTs hunched over, hard at work. Lyn stayed right where she was sitting, observing it all.

She watched as the frantic EMTs tried to push open the far door into the inner sanctum of Fayeville Hospital just as the magazine orderly was pushing a large rolling trash can back the other direction. The result was gridlock, and in the confusion that followed, the gurney was left briefly unattended. For the first time in many years, Lyn looked straight into the eyes of Travis Brayer.

He was on his back, but his neck was turned toward her and his eyes were open. His limbs were folded at odd angles and a gash on his head had bled down the side of his face. For a moment, Lyn thought he might even be dead, and she felt nothing but numbness. But then he blinked, and she realized he was still alive. Though she couldn't be sure just how conscious he actually was of what was happening.

Partly to test him and partly to amuse herself, she made her fingers into an imaginary gun and shot it in his direction. He closed his eyes, perhaps to protect himself from invisible bullets.

"You stay with us, Trav!" Roy Tomlins yelled.

Roy had struggled to keep up with all the commotion. He wasn't young or limber enough, but his concern for his friend infused him with adrenaline.

"Who's in charge here?" a younger, taller, broad-shouldered man asked in a loud, authoritative voice. "My dad needs care."

Bobby Brayer, Lyn realized. Everyone knew him from his campaign posters, but Lyn had also known him since he was a baby, when she'd worked at Brayer Plantation. She'd changed Bobby Brayer's diapers. And now here he was before her, a big man, running for governor and making a scene in a room that had just become too small.

The roadblock was sorted out, with the trash lady apologizing profusely in Spanish and flattening herself against the wall in a kind of prostrated position of penance to let them pass. With his eyes still sealed shut, Travis Brayer was rushed to the back, followed by his son and Roy Tomlins and one of the state troopers. Another of them stood guard at the door, glaring at the trash lady and putting up a hand to stop anyone else from trespassing where they shouldn't.

Lyn watched a curly-haired man in glasses try to talk his way past, to no avail. He took out his wallet and showed some laminated badges, but the state trooper seemed completely unmoved. Lyn watched the man accept defeat and seat himself near the door, where he was soon absorbed in leafing through his notebook, making occasional marks with his pen.

The hubbub had woken Jean and Walton, who were anxious to be filled in. Bo had left the room more than half an hour ago and was nowhere to be seen, which left Lyn with the responsibility of talking.

"What's happened?" Jean asked.

"Travis Brayer's had some kind of accident," Lyn replied in a monotone devoid of emotion.

"Oh my word, how awful," Jean gasped.

"I suppose so," Lyn replied mildly.

Jean gave her a sharp look. Lyn ignored this, but noticed that the curly-haired stranger was now only pretending to read his notebook while he actually listened to them.

"Well, is he okay? What was it?" Jean asked.

Lyn shook her head to convey that she didn't know, and didn't try to hide the possible implication that she didn't care.

"I only caught a glimpse," she replied.

She left out the fact that she had pantomimed shooting him in the face.

"I think this man was with him, though," Lyn continued, pointing out the stranger. "Maybe he knows."

The man immediately looked up in surprise, confirming Lyn's hunch that he had been listening closely. Jean and Walton turned to look at him.

"Walton Trawler, how do you do," Walton said as he crossed over and offered his hand in greeting.

"Oh, hello. I'm David Eisner," David said as he shook Walton's hand. "Nice to meet you."

"You a friend of the Brayers?" Walton inquired.

"Not exactly, no," David replied. "I'm a writer, doing a story on Bobby Brayer, among other people."

"Were you with them today? Were you there for the accident?" Jean asked anxiously.

"Yes, I was," David Eisner replied. "Mr. Brayer took a nasty fall and they're very concerned."

"Goodness," Jean said, shaking her head.

"How'd it happen?" Walton asked.

"Just an accident," David replied. "He got a little agitated and lost his footing. Are any of you familiar with the initials 'K.S.O.'?"

Lyn flinched and Jean stared at the ground. Only Walton held his gaze.

"Are they the initials of a Brayer relative or something?" David continued. "No 'B' obviously, but maybe from Bobby Brayer's mother's side of the family?"

"Is that what you were told?" Jean asked quickly.

Walton could see that Jean didn't want anyone to offer any explanation counter to whatever the Brayers might have already said. In her mind this was about sticking together as a community. Walton understood that mentality all too well, but he suddenly felt it was time for something different.

"It stands for Knights of the Southern Order," he told David Eisen.

Jean sucked in some air. "Walton," she said, with a warning tone in her voice.

Lyn had raised her head and Walton could feel her eyes on him.

"It's an offshoot of the Klan, started in this part of Mississippi over a hundred years ago."

David had frozen in surprise, an instinctive reaction he'd been trying to overcome for years, not least because it was an impediment to his chosen profession. When he should be scribbling or reaching for a cell phone camera shot or clicking on his tape recorder, he was frequently still and amazed, taking a costly moment to process some genuinely shocking development. It had led to him being regularly scooped as a cub reporter and was one of the reasons he'd begun focusing on longer form profiles.

"Really," David managed, goosing himself into action again. "And are the Brayers connected to the Knights of the Southern Order?"

"It's a secret society," Walton answered. "No one really knows who's connected or not, or even if anyone is at all anymore. It was mainly active forty years ago. You don't hear too much about it these days."

"Fascinating," David replied, as much to himself as anyone else.

He'd heard something about the fledgling investigation into the civil rights era crime here in Fayeville, and he'd asked Bobby Brayer about it. Bobby had assured him that should he be entrusted with the governorship he'd do everything in his power to punish any and all criminals. Other interviewees had talked about moving on from the past, but Bobby had been adamant that justice would be served, no matter how late. David wondered now if this was just another example of a politician speaking out loudest against things to which he or she felt some secret guilty connection. He'd seen this time and again: the closeted mayor denouncing gay marriage, the senator who solicited high-end call girls publicly railing against prostitution rings, the reform-obsessed committee chairwoman awash in bribes. Hypocrisy didn't surprise David. In fact, he'd come to expect it, which made it harder for genuine people to win him over.

"Kill Shootabay rides again," Lyn said softly.

Walton, Jean, and David all turned toward her. She looked startled, like she hadn't meant to speak aloud.

"Excuse me?" David asked.

"The Knights," Lyn replied. "We knew who they were. Even in their robes, you could still see their shoes."

She looked right at Walton, who felt deserving of the shame that engulfed him. He welcomed it even, grateful that there was some retribution after all, in a place where people had gotten away with everything.

Jean spoke up. "Some just thought of it as Southern pride."

Lyn stared at her.

"I'm not saying they were right," Jean continued defensively. "But to some it was just a rah-rah Southern patriotic thing. Partly."

The ensuing silence was its own rebuke. David looked from one to the other, enthralled by the tension.

"What was that name you said a second ago?" he asked Lyn, wishing he'd turned on his recorder faster. "You said someone rides again?"

"Kill Shootabay," Lyn answered. "People made him up—a monster that rides through town burning houses and snatching people. For the kids, to explain things when we had to. 'K.S.O.' would show up painted somewhere and we knew that someone was gonna be killed, probably shot, because they hadn't obeyed."

"Kill, Shoot, Obey," David repeated.

"I'd never heard that," Jean remarked.

Lyn ignored her.

"They killed my husband and daughter," she said to David.

"Oh my God, are you—?"

David couldn't remember the name. He knew about the case, and he'd asked Bobby Brayer about it, and now it was escaping him.

"Lyn Waters," Lyn said.

"Edward and Jiminy Waters!" David exclaimed.

Lyn winced, resenting their names being blurted out like a quiz show answer. It didn't feel like an improvement over their not being mentioned at all.

"Edward and Jiminy Waters," David repeated in a quieter voice. "Theirs is the case that might be reopened."

Lyn nodded.

"Do you know who did it?" David asked.

Lyn paused.

"I know it was the Knights," she said. "But I don't know which ones for sure. For all I know, the ones that did it might be long dead."

Jean stared out the window. She could see Bo in the hospital parking lot, bouncing a basketball hard against the pavement, as though he were trying to punish one or the other.

"Were any of the Brayers in K.S.O.?"

David posed this question to Lyn.

"Travis Brayer was," Lyn replied. "Don't know about his son."

"You don't know about Travis, either," Jean said automatically, unsure exactly why she felt compelled to protect him.

She'd never particularly liked Travis Brayer, though she'd admired his wealth and standing. Travis had enjoyed her husband Floyd, as everyone had, and he'd always invited Floyd and Jean to Brayer Plantation parties. He'd given them reasons to dress up, which injected excitement into otherwise dull routines. Jean recognized that this was a frivolous reason to defend him, particularly against something indefensible.

"Travis Brayer's a Knight," Walton said softly but clearly. "There aren't many who weren't, me included. And it's past time we answered for it."

His admission reshuffled the air around all of them. It blew through the room, and facts settled like leaves in its wake.

Part Three

JIMINY STOOD AT THE EDGE of the courthouse steps and scanned the lawn for Bo, whom she felt a bit desperate to find. She wanted to talk to him, alone, away from everything and everyone else. When they were together, she'd felt more like herself than she had her whole life, and she longed again for that sensation.

Disappointed not to spot him, she sank down beside the memorial for Fayeville soldiers killed in battle, closed her eyes, and turned her face sunward.

She tried to clear her mind, determined to have a little part of this day for herself only. A little sunny, quiet part. She needed to sort some things out.

A few minutes later, she sensed someone standing over her. She smiled without opening her eyes.

"Where have you been?" she asked.

It took a lot of willpower to keep her eyes closed, but she hoped the effect was confident and sexy. She wanted Bo to want her back.

"Meeting with the clerk," Carlos answered.

Jiminy's eyes flew open in surprise.

"Oh! Hi!" she exclaimed.

Carlos laughed.

"Expecting someone else?" he asked.

Jiminy blushed.

"I'm happy it's you," she replied.

This was sincere. She really liked Carlos. Nothing physical had happened between them since the night he'd almost kissed her, and Jiminy didn't plan for them to be anything other than friendly colleagues. But the alternatives hovered, quickening the pulse between them. She felt them in the way he looked at her, in his crooked smile.

"Busy?" Carlos asked.

"Deeply. Can't you tell?"

He lay down in the grass next to her, leaning back on his elbows.

"This is the best part of my day so far," he said.

The night they'd been interrupted by the ambulance whisking Jiminy's grandmother past them to the hospital, when Walton had spotted them and pulled over his car to tell them what was happening, Carlos had watched Jiminy struggle to process the news. He'd watched her blame and then absolve herself, all amid shock and grief. He'd fallen a little for her in that moment. His ex-wife would say it was because of the drama and the sirens and the overall chaos. She'd say the turmoil was what he was attracted to, and that he was simply cultivating affection for a woman who could conveniently embody it. And if that was true, then he would tire of Jiminy once the excitement had passed. He didn't plan to overtly pursue her; he intended to focus on the work at hand. But her company was a pleasant perk of the job, and he allowed himself to imagine further possibilities.

"Any luck today?" she asked.

They'd run into roadblock after roadblock trying to persuade various Fayevillians to speak openly about what had happened to the Waters. Thus far, the defunct 1966 almanac had been more forthcoming about what may or may not have transpired that year than any living breathing human had. People didn't even want to discuss what the weather had been like, or the crop yield. They just went silent and blank. Some seemed ashamed, others depressed, a few defiant. A surprising number seemed amnesiac.

Carlos sighed.

"None to speak of. You?"

Jiminy shook her head.

"No. Though I can't get my mind off of those photos, especially the self-portrait of my granddad and the shot of Lyn. There's something so haunting about them," she said.

"You and your pictures," Carlos replied.

Jiminy took Polaroids of everyone they spoke to—quickly and without asking permission. It often caused immediate discomfort, but Jiminy couldn't help herself. Carlos had given up trying to dissuade her. At night, she arranged the photos across her bed in a celluloid lineup.

But it was the album of her grandfather's decades-old photos that continued to preoccupy her. Carlos had threatened to confiscate it, to force her to focus on activities that might actually advance their case. Jiminy thought of this now, as the sun beat down on them. She felt herself getting overheated.

"Can we get out of here?" she asked.

"Absolutely," Carlos replied.

He stood and pulled her up after him. Just ahead of them, Bo walked out of the library. For a split second, Jiminy simply froze. Then she dropped Carlos's hand to move toward Bo.

"There you are!" she exclaimed.

"Hi," Bo said, in a tone that stopped her short of the hug she might have been going for.

He hadn't meant to sound so curt. Bo had seen the look that crossed Jiminy's face when she'd spotted him. It had been thrilled and confused and worried all at once. But he'd also seen her holding hands with Carlos, and now he just needed to get away from them. He didn't want to hate Carlos, or resent Jiminy, or second-guess himself. He wanted to be bigger than all of those emotions.

"I've been looking for you," Jiminy said.

Bo stayed silent.

"I've actually gotta check on something in the library," Carlos interjected as he moved easily past them.

Jiminy kept her eyes trained on Bo.

"I need to talk to you."

Bo heard the plea in her voice, but didn't let himself weaken.

"I can't now, I've gotta get somewhere," he replied.

Jiminy nodded slowly, upset. They both were.

"So you must've taken the MCATs," she said. "Congratulations."

"I won't know how I did for a while, but thanks," he answered.

They stood looking at each other, hamstrung by awkwardness.

"I really miss you," Jiminy blurted.

She was embarrassed, then resolved.

"I do," she continued with a shrug. "A lot. I miss being with you. I know you don't think we can be together in this place, but I just want you to know that I wish things were different. I'm trying to make them different."

Bo took this in, swallowed, breathed.

"Thanks," he replied. "But you seem to have moved on pretty well."

Confusion flashed through her features. Despite himself, Bo felt an urge to lift his hand and trace the outline of her lips. He looked away.

"I really do need to get going," he said.

"You've got the wrong idea," Jiminy protested. "There's nothing—"

"I gotta go, J," Bo interrupted. "It's okay, it's all okay."

He smiled to cover the ache he felt, then moved past her, close enough to smell her coconut hair. He held his breath until he was in the clear.

W ALTON HADN'T INTENDED to abuse his ongoing privileges at the hospital to sneak into Travis Brayer's room. Still, there he found himself, sitting bedside, scribbling in his notebook and looking at his old friend.

As he watched Travis sleep, Walton thought back to the night when he'd been brought the bodies of Edward and Jiminy, and Henry had implored him to treat them with the dignity he'd show any others. Any others who were white, he'd meant.

"There's no difference," Henry said.

"Of course there's a difference," Walton argued. "And you know the boys won't like it if I do this. Edward and Jiminy are gone, their people will bury them, that's it."

"No," Henry said fiercely. "This matters."

"I know you were close," Walton said, putting his hand on Henry's shoulder. "I know he was almost like a brother to you—"

"Do you?" Henry interrupted. "Do you really have any idea how close we were?"

Walton looked away, at anywhere but into Henry's furious, anguished face.

"And Jiminy—" Henry exclaimed, his voice cracking.

This was the moment Walton had decided to agree, to help, to do no further harm. He'd set about cleaning and dressing Edward's and Jiminy's wounds, keeping his head bent, aware that Henry was watching silently, tears pouring down his face.

Walton hadn't quite finished when Lyn came into the room, but he'd at least made them presentable—if it's even possible to make the bodies of loved ones presentable to people who only want them to be alive.

Considering how Lyn behaved, Walton was relieved that he hadn't let her see her husband and daughter when they'd been in any worse shape. Henry had been right: this mattered. There was no difference.

He watched Lyn's excruciating reaction, and how Henry moved instinctively for her, as much to comfort himself as to offer support. She wanted none of him, that much she made clear. Her rejection was absolute. And unthinkable under any other circumstances. When she'd left the room, Henry collapsed against the wall, wracked with shuddering sobs.

Walton hadn't known what to do. He waited for Henry to collect himself, which took an uncomfortably long time. Then Edward's brother came to retrieve the bodies, and Henry helped move them out to the car. Henry never said goodbye to Walton that night; he simply came over and wordlessly took Walton's hand in his.

Less than a year later, at the age of thirty-two, Henry was dead. Walton had seen his body as well, and it had also been too late. He'd been asked to perform an autopsy to help discover what had killed a man so young and seemingly healthy. He found the giant blockage in the main artery close to the heart, wrote "massive pulmonary embolism" in the chart, and sewed up the incision he'd made, with a sense of wonder and loss. Literally seeing the insides of men changed a person's perspective. Walton thought about this as he stitched up the body. He thought of many things. Of whether this blockage had started as a tiny speck the night Henry had sobbed and raged and been rejected by Lyn. Of whether there was any way to see this death as a blessing. Of what would happen to

Willa now; and to their daughter, Margaret, the little girl he'd delivered; and to Lyn, who had emotionally shut herself down even though she technically remained among the living. But most of all, he thought about how much Henry felt like Edward to the touch.

Walton remembered this now, as he stared at Travis Brayer's sleeping form. He resisted an urge to reach out his hand to feel Travis's skin. To get a sense of the shape of his muscles and bones, beneath what everyone saw on the surface. He wanted to do this, and he wanted Travis to wake up.

Suddenly, stridently, the phone on the bedside table rang. Startled, Walton picked it up.

"Trav?" a familiar voice asked from the other end.

"No, he's sleeping," Walton replied.

"Walton? Is that you?"

Walton recognized Roy Tomlins's voice.

"Hey, Roy," he replied. "I'm glad you called."

"What's going on there?"

"Just sitting here with Trav, scribbling down everything I remember about June of '66," Walton replied.

Roy stayed silent.

"Remember that month?" Walton continued. "We were all upset about the marches. Folks wanted to drive over to Jackson and shoot that Meredith boy. I remember you showing off which shotgun you'd use."

"I don't recollect that, Walton. Tell Trav it's me calling."

"And we were outraged that Jiminy Waters had dared to enter that state leadership essay contest, remember? How'd we even find out that she submitted something? She mailed it I guess. Did you open her letter, Roy? Did she drop it off herself at the post office, or did Edward?"

"Put Trav on the phone, Walton."

"I told you, he's asleep. But I'll be sure to give him the message."

Walton hung up the phone just as Travis started to stir. Walton wondered how much he'd heard or understood, if any at all. He thought about how easy it would be to turn off the machine that was keeping him alive. He knew exactly which switches to flip.

"Can you hear me, Travis?" Walton asked.

Travis nodded, a shaved-head little-boy nod.

"Good," Walton replied. "Because we have a lot to discuss."

THE DRIVE TO Bo's great-uncle's house was more painful alone in the daylight. Weeks ago, with Jiminy next
to him in the darkness, everything about it had seemed
surprising and fun. The woman by his side, the roughness of
the hill road, the shock of the nocturnal animals they'd spot-
lighted along the way. Now it just seemed dusty and lonely
and way too bright. Bo wished he hadn't agreed to visit. He
wished he'd said no, that it wasn't a good time. But he'd been
caught off guard and agreed instead, and now he was pulling
up to his uncle Fred's cabin under much more depressing circumstances.

Fred was scattering chicken feed on the dirt outside the coop.
At first glance, it seemed that creatures ran wild on Fred's property, but in reality there was some control to the chaos. He had
a system he'd worked out that he described as being "in cahoots
with the critters," and it was true that among them he seemed
to be part of a happy, raucous commune. As Bo approached, he
looked up and grinned a toothless grin.

"Right on time for some lemony-lime," he said.

Bo wasn't sure what he meant until he saw the iced jug on
the table in the front yard. Fred liked to invent different cold
drinks in the summer, using whatever he could gather fresh
from his garden or the nearby woods. This wasn't the climate
for lemons or limes, but Bo thought he saw some mint leaves
and apple chunks floating in the punch.

He took a cautious sip from the glass jar Fred offered him.

"Whew," Bo said, wiping his lip and setting the jar back on
the table.

He'd been right about the mint. He couldn't be sure about the apples, because whatever fruit they'd once been, they were now just little sponges for whiskey.

"Lemony-lime moonshine mint punch," Fred proclaimed proudly.

"That's something," Bo answered.

Fred was a man of many projects, which Bo found intriguing. He was well into his eighties, and he lived a solitary, reclusive life. He could've just faded away from sense and sensibility the way he'd shied from other people, but he'd instead managed to stay engaged and alert. In addition to being a little kooky, Fred was filled with an energy that Bo admired.

"Where's Lily-Lou?" Fred asked.

By which he meant Jiminy. He'd started calling her that when they were all together weeks ago. He'd said there was only one Jiminy he'd ever known, and so this other Jiminy must be Lily-Lou. Wanting to know all she could about the other Jiminy, the newly christened Lily-Lou had gracefully played along.

"I'm not too sure," Bo answered, wondering if his uncle could leave it at that.

"You've lost Lily-Lou?" Fred gasped. "You don't know where to find her?"

Nope, Bo guessed that he couldn't just leave it at that.

"We're not spending as much time together anymore."

Fred nodded.

"Trouble with the Knights," he said.

He didn't ask it. He just said it. Bo didn't know what he meant, but he tried to go along to get along.

"With the days, too," Bo replied. "It's for the best. She shouldn't have to deal with any trouble while she figures herself out, and I'm gonna be leaving town again soon anyway."

"You still lookin' out for Jiminy?" Fred asked. "And Edward, too? They're a pair forever and ever now, till reincarnation do them part."

He was talking about the first Jiminy. The second one was still Lily-Lou.

"Of course," Bo said. "Though it's really Jiminy—I mean, it's really Lily-Lou who's gotten obsessed with them. She's gone and gotten someone to come make a real investigation, to really dig into it. They're creating quite a stir."

"I knew it, I knew it," Fred said, clapping his hands to his knees. "When they want some ammudence, tell 'em to come see Fred."

Bo thought about it for a moment but couldn't decipher the word.

"Ammudence?"

"Ammudence!" Fred repeated. "When they need some fire that'll really stick, proof and power all in one!"

Ammunition. And evidence?

"What do you have?" Bo asked.

And why hadn't Fred mentioned it weeks ago when they'd first visited him? Perhaps their questions had awakened old memories that he'd needed a little time alone with before feeling ready to act.

Bo had been horrified to learn what had happened to Edward and Jiminy, but he'd never personally known them. He knew his great-aunt Lyn as well as she let anyone know her, and he sympathized deeply with her, but overall, he felt removed from the long-ago events that had shattered her. And, in truth, he didn't want to be saddled with all the baggage from them. He wanted to move forward into his own future, away from this place where the burdens of past generations, though unknown and invisible, somehow still retained the power to hold the next generation down.

But Jiminy's obsession with his family's past had shamed Bo into further investigation. For better or for worse, he'd been drafted.

"You wanna see some ammudence?" Fred asked him. "Follow me."

In the yard, two peacocks strutted among the chickens. Worried that he might accidentally squash a chick, Bo stepped carefully as he followed Fred to a falling-down barn nestled against the hillside behind the house.

"Thisaway," Fred said, ducking under a listing beam to enter the barn.

Inside, Fred walked toward a stall at the far end. He struggled to move a bale of hay blocking its entrance, and Bo hurried to help him, happy that his youth was good for something. Fred squeezed into the opening they'd made and pointed into the shadows of the stall. It took a moment for Bo's eyes to make out what looked like a heap of something covered in dusty canvas.

Bo swatted a fly and stepped into the stall to get a better view as Fred lifted the tarp away. It seemed to be the rusted-up, burned-out front of a car, complete with charred seats and steering wheel. Bo looked at Fred, understanding dawning on him.

"Their car?" Bo asked. "The car they were driving that night?"

Fred nodded.

"It didn't burn all the way up. I got it in the middle of the night and've had it since. Maybe now's its time to shine."

Bo nodded, suddenly unable to speak. Seeing these charred remains before him made what had transpired real in a way that nothing else had. He no longer just felt sorry for Lyn, or horror in general. He felt as if this had somehow happened to him.

"Maybe it's the perfect ammudence," Fred said.

"So it looks like a trial is really going to happen," Jiminy said quietly. "With the Brayer connection and the governor's race, there's a lot of pressure to see if there's anything to all this. It could happen really quickly."

Lyn nodded, keeping her thoughts to herself. "Quickly" was an extremely relative term.

Jiminy had found her on Willa's side porch steps, eating her lunch in the shade. She'd just sat down and started talking, not bothering to ask if Lyn wanted company.

"The car could play a key role," she continued. "The FBI's ordered DNA testing."

Lyn didn't want to think about that. She knew it could be helpful, but she didn't want to revisit the specter of the people she'd loved most in the world being part of violence that had spilled and snagged and crushed and torn, leaving little pieces of them behind. She set her plate on the ground, willfully surrendering it to the ants.

"Are you okay?" Jiminy asked.

Lyn stared at her, noting that her face was darker from time spent in the sun, and that there was something more certain about her features. Willa and Henry's granddaughter seemed to be settling into her body, slowly and steadily.

"I mean, I'm sorry if you didn't want any of this," Jiminy continued. "I should have been more sensitive about that."

Lyn recognized that in addition to the physical changes, Jiminy was nowhere near as hesitant as she'd been when she'd first arrived. And despite her intrusiveness, or maybe because of it, Lyn appreciated her.

"This needed to happen," Lyn said simply.

Jiminy took this in, and nodded slowly. After a moment, she reached into her bag.

"I'd like to show you something," she said.

She'd made some copies of her grandfather's photos. Carlos had reprimanded her for her preoccupation with her family's personal connection to the case they were investigating, but what if that link held some valuable key? What if, in the end, it was the whole point?

Jiminy handed Lyn a copy of the photo of her that had been taken over forty years before. Lyn held it lightly, examining her younger self.

"Do you remember when that was taken?" Jiminy asked. "It seems like some kind of occasion."

Lyn gazed a bit longer, then shrugged.

"Your grandpa was always taking photos," she replied. "I was bound to be in one eventually."

Jiminy handed her a copy of the photograph of her grandfather.

"What about this one?" she asked. "I thought it was a self-portrait, but I found out they didn't have timers back then. Do you know who might've taken it?"

Lyn glanced at it, then shook her head.

"No idea." she replied.

Jiminy nodded.

"Well, I couldn't stop looking at it when I saw it," she said. "He looks so sad, and so old for thirty-two. I couldn't stop staring at his eyes."

The hazel eyes that she'd inherited. Her grandfather had

worn glasses, and the sunlight was glinting off their edges in the photo, winking at the camera.

"There just seemed like there was more of a story there," Jiminy continued. "So I took it to the photo zone at HushMart and got a little help, and sure enough, there was something."

Jiminy handed another photograph to Lyn. In this one, the eyes filled the entire sheet, and their magnified proportions revealed that the reflection in Henry's glasses that had initially seemed like clouds or trees was actually a person, sitting opposite, holding a camera. Henry's gigantic eyes were mirrors that showed a young Lyn snapping his photo.

"Does that help you remember?" Jiminy asked.

Lyn met Jiminy's gaze.

"I think it's time we took a ride together," Lyn said.

———

A short time later, Jiminy was standing, hushed, holding her hand to her mouth. She closed her eyes reverently, then opened them again to gaze at the etched gravestones. One read "Edward Waters—beloved husband." The other simply said "Sweet Jiminy."

Lyn was standing beside her, swaying ever so slightly, like a sturdy tree in a strong breeze.

"This is a church," Jiminy said reverently. "You're a church."

Indeed, as often happened when Lyn communed with her lost ones, she felt filled with something holy.

"Listen to what I tell you," she replied. "Because I'll only say it once."

Jiminy nodded. She felt like she might be falling into some sort of trance.

"Your grandfather had more than one daughter."

It was almost as though Lyn was telling her a bedtime story.

"He had your mother with Willa," she continued. "But before that, he had another daughter. With me."

Jiminy remained completely still. She didn't even breathe.

"My Jiminy was your mother's half sister, your grandpa's first daughter, born five years before he even met your grandma."

Now Jiminy blinked rapidly as her brain whirled into action. She didn't feel as shocked as she thought she should. It was almost as though she'd known all along. She couldn't have, she realized, yet still, that was the feeling. She needed to hear more.

"Does my grandma know?" she asked quietly.

Lyn sighed.

"We've never discussed it, and Henry never told her far as I know," she replied. "But I think she figured it out."

Jiminy nodded.

"It was an accident . . . a mistake," Lyn said.

She closed her eyes a moment, then took a long, slow breath.

"I was in St. Louis, preparing to leave my sister and my folks and move down here to marry Edward," she continued. "Edward and I fell for each other quick and didn't see a point in waiting. I knew we belonged together within a minute of seeing him. Edward used to say it took him a minute and a half, but that I was always a step or two ahead of him."

Jiminy smiled. She liked romantic stories about other people's courtships. They were her favorite kind of fairy tale.

"By this point, Edward was living on Henry's farm and they'd started their carpentry business. One of the Brayer cousins bought a place in St. Louis and wanted a replica of the dining room table and chairs at Brayer Plantation, so he hired Henry to take the measurements and start the job."

"Okay," Jiminy said, struggling to keep the judgment from her voice. "And you and Edward were engaged."

"Till Henry got to St. Louis we were," Lyn replied sadly. "But he brought a letter for me from Edward that broke it off. It said I shouldn't come to Mississippi, that I'd have a better life in St. Louis, that I should go on along without him."

"Why?" Jiminy asked.

"He didn't say. My folks figured I'd done something wrong and kicked me out. Which is when I did do something wrong."

"You slept with Henry," Jiminy said softly.

Lyn looked off in the distance, at the rolling hills and the many bends in the river.

"Once. And hated myself afterwards. Then Edward showed up the next day asking for me back."

"Oh God, why'd he break it off in the first place?"

Lyn closed her eyes for another long moment.

"The K.S.O. burned his mother's house the week before, and he said it didn't feel safe or right to bring me down to Fayeville to live. He said he loved me too much to have me be in a place that would only cause suffering."

"Why didn't he just leave himself?" Jiminy asked. "You guys could've lived in St. Louis, or anywhere."

Jiminy felt the same sense of frustrated agitation she got when she watched *Romeo and Juliet* or *Titanic*—she desperately wanted to alter an unchangeable ending. Lyn shook her head.

"He had to stay in Fayeville to look after his mother and be close to his brothers and sisters. He wanted me, but he understood if I wouldn't come."

"And you obviously told him you would."

"I married him that day," Lyn said.

"So Jiminy could still have been Edward's daughter, then,"

Jiminy exclaimed. "I mean, Edward could have been the father just as easily as my grandpa."

Again, Lyn shook her head.

"I couldn't ever get pregnant again," she said. "We tried for seventeen years. Jiminy was Henry's."

Jiminy took a moment to absorb this.

"So what did my grandpa do?" she asked. "Nothing?"

Lyn sighed.

"We only spoke of it once, which was plenty. He blamed me for marrying Edward after what we'd done. Told me I was fickle and immoral, and that Edward deserved better."

"But you really did love Edward," Jiminy said.

"More than anything in this world," Lyn replied. "I woulda done anything to erase what happened with Henry. Anything. I kept it secret, and I don't think Edward ever suspected. Folks said his real father was a white man who'd raped his mother, so he always believed this accounted for Jiminy's lighter skin. And make no mistake, Edward was Jiminy's father in every other way that mattered."

"How did my grandpa treat Jiminy?"

"He loved her. Doted on her, to tell the truth, which made Edward so proud. It was me Henry hated."

"He really never forgave you?"

"Not till it was too late," Lyn replied. "He never wanted me around. Made me get another job at the Brayers even, which . . ."

As Lyn trailed off, Jiminy looked over at her quickly.

She pressed: "Which what?"

Lyn crossed her arms to hug herself.

"Which is when everything went wrong."

Lyn shook her head slowly, and Jiminy wondered how she could possibly carry so much pain around with her every day.

"What do you mean?" she asked softly. "What went wrong?"
Lyn stared at the river far below them.

"Travis Brayer took an interest in me, and Travis Brayer don't like bein' told no."

Jiminy felt suddenly and deeply chilled. She shivered violently.

"Henry felt awful about it," Lyn continued in a detached monotone. "After Edward and Jiminy were killed, he just fell apart. He didn't know how to make sense of any of it; he didn't know how to grieve. He just got worse and worse. He asked me to take that photograph of him in December of '66, right before Christmas. We came here to take it."

Jiminy looked at the photo again. It was true; it had been taken right where she was now standing. She could see the magnolia branch above her grandfather's head and the edge of Edward's gravestone beside him.

"He told me it was important that I take the photo, that we needed a record," Lyn continued. "He was a little out of his mind then, searching for something he couldn't find. And then he just broke."

Jiminy stayed very still, trying to imagine what her grandfather must have been feeling, standing here, over four decades earlier.

"He'd lost a close friend, and his daughter," Jiminy said, almost to herself. "My mother's half sister—my aunt . . ."

The full weight of this impacted her. She and Jiminy Waters shared more than just a name. They shared blood.

Jiminy looked at Lyn.

"Which makes you my . . ."

She stopped. This was getting too confusing. No, Lyn wasn't

actually related to her, she quickly worked out. And thankfully, neither was Bo. But they were all tangled up in the same web.

"So now you know," Lyn said. "I'd just as soon the Henry part stay between us. For Edward's sake."

Jiminy nodded slowly.

"I won't tell, but with the DNA testing, it's hard to say what might come out," Jiminy replied.

Lyn nodded, resigned to being disappointed. Jiminy ached for her. She ached for all of them. Things got so complicated when blood was involved.

O F ALL THE MANY THINGS Willa could be worrying about, she found herself preoccupied with the whereabouts of Jiminy's kitten. Cholera had slipped out the window per her normal routine, to hunt or wander, but failed to return, and had now been missing for several days. Perhaps a coyote had carried her off in the night. Perhaps she'd left of her own free will. When someone or something disappeared, did the reasons really matter all that much in the end? People yearned to sweeten absence with explanations, Willa knew. But did they provide any real, lasting solace? In her opinion, the jury was out.

Still, Willa missed Cholera. She'd never before allowed live animals in her house, because she'd been raised to keep them outside, to maintain some separation between human and beast. In a family as poor as hers had been, the distinction had been important. But she'd made an exception for Cholera, because she'd come to welcome her visits. The first one had happened the day after Willa returned from the hospital to recuperate at home. The kitten slunk into the bedroom and leapt up onto the mattress, where she stretched and used her little claws to knead the blanket like it was dough for biscuits. Willa could feel the tiny pricks on her skin below, but she hadn't cried out or shifted. She'd just watched the kitten settle into the little space she'd kneaded for herself, and reflected that that's what you did with a bed that you made. You lay in it.

Willa heard the front door close and wondered whether it was Lyn, Jiminy, or Jean. Jean had moved into the farmhouse to help tend to Willa's recovery, though she spent an equal amount of time playing virtual tennis in the room down the hall.

"Yoo-hoo," Willa called.

"It's me, Grandma," Jiminy answered, entering Willa's bedroom from the hall. "We need to talk."

———

Half an hour later, Willa longed to rest her brain and eyes, but her granddaughter was still asking questions. Intensive conversation was new terrain for them, and even had Willa been in perfect health, she wasn't sure she'd have been up for it.

Jiminy hadn't shared anything that Lyn had told her. Her aim was to gather information rather than dispense it, and to that end, she'd been peppering her grandmother with queries about the past, claiming curiosity about her mother's childhood. Jiminy had calculated that Willa would be more forthcoming if she believed Jiminy was simply trying to understand just what exactly had gone wrong with her mother.

So far, the strategy was proving fruitful. In response to Jiminy's probing, Willa had tried her best to explain how much Margaret had worshiped the first Jiminy, and how fiercely she'd mourned her and Edward's deaths. Willa had admitted she'd lied about the circumstances of their deaths at the time, ascribing them to a tragic car accident in an attempt to shield her young daughter a bit longer from the devastating actuality of the world.

Willa remembered clearly how Margaret had cocked her little head and pronounced her a liar. Apparently she had been eavesdropping outside Willa and Henry's door right after the bodies were found, and had heard her father sob and rage and ask desperately how anyone could do such things to another human being. She'd heard him declare he didn't want to be on a planet that condoned this, in a life where this went on. Margaret had been haunted by his words, both at the time and years afterward, whenever she'd thought about her father's premature death. She felt she'd witnessed the exact moment he'd decided to leave.

Jiminy listened carefully as her grandmother relayed all of this in her thin, tired voice.

"So maybe that's why Mom decided she'd prefer an alternate world, too," Jiminy said. "And after her car accident, after the pills took over, she finally fully went for it. She cracked and went for it."

And had proceeded to live an irresponsible life on her own selfish terms. But who were they to question this, in the end? Maybe it was the only way to be.

"She's not completely unaware, you know," Willa said. "She called the other day. And she sent this."

Willa indicated a package resting on her bedside table that Jiminy hadn't even noticed. It was addressed to her, mailed from a Greek seaport.

Jiminy picked it up and tore open an end. A mound of bubble wrap slipped out into her lap. Buried within its many layers was the wooden doll she'd played with in her youth. The beautifully carved boy who'd once been her constant companion.

"It's him," she breathed.

He was accompanied by a note:

Cricket,

Remember this guy? You never lost him—he's been with me—I take him on all my trips. He was mine first, you know. Edward made him for Jiminy, and Jiminy gave him to me. He was only on loan to you, but I figured you could use his company now.

Love, Mom

Jiminy let the note fall to her lap. Gazing at her long-lost little cohort triggered strange sensations of forgotten times when her brain had still been maturing and she'd thought wooden objects could spring to life. The sensations seemed pleasant at first, but they were unsettling, too. As she ran her fingers over the little wooden boy's limbs, she felt as though she were regressing.

"He came back," she said softly.

After all this time, now that she had a fully formed brain no longer comforted by magical thinking.

Gunshots interrupted her reunion. Jiminy jumped, but her grandmother stayed remarkably serene.

"It's just Jean," Willa said calmly. "She must've lost another game."

Jiminy went to the window, where she saw Jean aiming her rifle at something she'd perched on the fence post. Jiminy squinted. Sure enough, it looked like one of the videogame consoles Jean had brought with her and hooked up to the television when she'd moved into Willa's. She'd been playing tennis against the machine every day for exercise, but apparently the latest match hadn't gone well.

"She really hates losing," Willa explained.

Didn't they all.

―――――

Carlos wasn't at the courthouse like he'd said he'd be, so Jiminy decided to try his room at the Comfort Inn. She was eager to pursue the leads she'd uncovered, armed with the insight she'd acquired. As she rapped on Carlos's door, she tried to calm her jiggling leg. She wondered if she wasn't also a little excited to see Carlos himself.

From inside, she heard muffled murmurs and hurried rustling.

"One second," Carlos called.

Perhaps she'd caught him napping. They'd been battling a sense of impatient frustration lately, haunted by the worry that they were running out of time. The car discovery had provided fresh momentum for their case, but unless they could come up with positive DNA matches, it wasn't going to help them prosecute anyone.

Adding to their angst was the fact that Carlos had begun receiving a significant amount of pressure from people associated with Bobby Brayer's gubernatorial campaign to back off the case altogether, and though he was impervious to such influence, he worried that the law enforcement agencies he relied on might not be. He had emphasized to Jiminy that they needed to crack something soon.

Jiminy knew that Carlos meditated to work through thorny problems, and that this practice often led to unplanned naps. She hadn't meant to interrupt or embarrass him.

Sure enough, he was barefoot and rumpled when he cracked open his door a moment later. Jiminy had an unsettling urge to crawl into bed with him.

"Everything okay?" he asked.

"Everything's great—I'm sorry to bother you," Jiminy began.

"I gotta go anyway," a woman's voice said from behind Carlos.

She was tan with frosted blond hair. She looked familiar, but Jiminy couldn't place where she'd previously seen her.

"I was just interviewing Gloria," Carlos explained.

The woman laughed a smoker's husky cackle.

"Yeah, I hope you got what you needed," she said, swatting Carlos's butt as she breezed out the door. She didn't look at Jiminy as she passed. She just straightened the straps of her dress, donned her sunglasses, and strode toward the parking lot. Jiminy watched her go, still too surprised to speak.

Carlos cleared his throat.

"What's going on?" he asked.

Jiminy refocused her attention on him. He was leaning against the door frame, observing her. In his gray T-shirt, with his limbs akimbo, he reminded her of a spider. Jiminy thought of all the times she'd used a glass and a sheet of paper to trap in lieu of squashing.

"We need to get to Travis Brayer," she said brusquely. "You seem busy, so I'll give it a shot myself."

Her voice sounded different to her—more solid and sure. She wondered if this new confidence also showed in her stance and posture, and in the look she was giving Carlos now. Appraising, rather than seeking or questioning. She was hardening into her actual self all on her own, she could feel it.

"That'll be delicate," Carlos said slowly. "I should be there. I've just got one more interview here and then I'm free. Wait for me."

Jiminy heard a car easing into the Comfort Inn parking lot and turned to see the librarian parking, looking toward Carlos expectantly. Her hair was curled, and she was wearing bright red lipstick.

Jiminy took her Polaroid camera from her bag and snapped a photo of Carlos.

"I'll let you know how it goes," she said, before turning and walking away.

In her car as she was driving off, the picture of Carlos slowly came into focus. Jiminy contemplated it, and the road ahead, without looking back.

FROM HIS PERCH AT GRADY'S GRILL, Walton saw Willa's car glide by, driven by Jiminy, who seemed in a hurry. Walton wondered what lives she was racing to upend next. He certainly recognized the role she'd played in rattling his. Without her, he never would have committed his darkest secrets to paper.

He stubbed out his cigarette, pleased at the symmetry of ending it along with his latest, most essential project, and gathered his manuscript as he pondered what to do. He'd written a definitive history of the Waters murders, complete with a confession. He'd determined to be painfully, importantly honest, and now he was done.

He might share this loaded document with the rest of the world, or he might burn it. He hadn't made up his mind.

Outside, storm clouds were gathering to the north and the air felt charged. Walton glanced to his right and saw Carlos standing on the upper balcony of the Comfort Inn, staring off down the road. Nearby, Tortillas looked as though it had been shut down, and Walton felt his reawakened impulse to investigate. "Curiosity killed the cat," ran through his head in the warning voice of his late father. "Satisfaction brought her back," chimed the answer at its heels.

———

A short time later, Walton was yelling Carlos's name as he limped hurriedly across the Comfort Inn parking lot. Carlos took the stairs down two at a time to meet him, concerned by the agitation in the old man's voice.

When they got to Tortillas, the door was still ajar, the way Walton had left it. Inside, the place was a mix of orderliness and chaos. The chairs had been put up on the tables in preparation for the floor to be mopped, but there was nothing clean about what lay beneath them. For a moment, Carlos thought it was blood, but he was relieved to see a can of red spray paint discarded in a corner of the room. Whoever had done this must have used more than one can, though. The floor was covered with spray paint outlines of bodies, the kind that are normally drawn in chalk at crime scenes. There were dozens of them, covering every inch of Tortillas floor space. They even climbed up the walls with a splayed limb here or there, in a way that would have struck Carlos as artistic if the whole thing hadn't been so grotesque.

Inside each of the bodies was a name. Carlos read some of them, unaware that he was pronouncing them aloud.

"Juan Gonzalez. Rosa Gonzalez. Penelope Gonzalez. Maria Gonzalez. Paco Hernandez. Teresa Hernandez. Guillermo Lopez. Isabella Lopez."

"These are real people," Walton said behind him. "Juan and Rosa own this restaurant. Or they did."

The place looked like it had been left in a hurry. Above the doorway to the kitchen, "Care of K.S.O." had been spray-painted in large, red letters.

"Who are the others?" Carlos asked, waving his hand over the outlines of dozens of labeled bodies.

Walton shook his head.

"I don't know."

Carlos nodded. His stomach felt hollow.

"But they're why I'm giving this to you," Walton said, handing over the stack of papers he'd been carrying. "I have to. This can't go on."

Carlos was still staring around him at all the hypothetical bodies, unaware of the significance of Walton's decision—oblivious that the horror around them had inspired a momentous atonement.

"Let's get out of here," he said sharply.

There was nothing Walton wanted to do more.

I N THE HOSPITAL PARKING LOT, Rosa balanced her baby on one hip while closing the car door with her other. She didn't have much time, and she needed to be certain that Pen was healthy enough to undertake a long journey. Juan's cousin who worked at the hospital had promised to help.

Rosa was surprised by Jiminy at the emergency room door—they nearly collided before engaging in the kind of pass-attempt shuffle dance that occasionally delays people for longer than seems reasonable. They kept choosing the same direction, only to simultaneously readjust to the same alternate one. Back and forth they went, in a box step of starts and stops.

"I'm sorry, you pass," Jiminy said, stopping the shuffling before it reached a point of total ridiculousness.

Jiminy had come to the hospital to seek access to Travis Brayer, only to be informed that he'd been checked out by his family an hour before. Which meant he was back at Brayer Plantation, surrounded by guards and minders. Jiminy couldn't shake the feeling that she'd missed an important window of opportunity, and this frustrated her. She could sense the clock running out, and for the first time, she wondered about the hubris of expecting a happy ending. She'd hoped at the very least that an investigation would bring some kind of clarity and redemption, but what if it didn't? What if it did nothing? Or made everything worse?

As she stood back for Rosa to pass, her mind flashed to the empanada and beer night when Carlos had nearly kissed her, and she felt a yearning for Bo. She sighed without realizing it, causing Rosa to look at her.

"How's the restaurant?" Jiminy asked, to cover up her fool-ishness.

Rosa glanced downward.

"We're closed," she replied.

Pen began howling, as if on cue. Rosa jiggled her up and down as she avoided Jiminy's gaze.

"We're leaving," Rosa continued. "We have to leave."

There was no reason to elaborate about why they were leav-ing, Rosa decided. No reason to describe how this place had become so ugly for them. Even after traveling all this way and laying down a foundation and starting a business and having a baby and carving out a better life than the one they'd left . . . in the end, it wasn't enough. Once you'd been beaten in a town, you'd been beaten by a town. They had to go elsewhere. Juan had some relatives in North Carolina who were encouraging them to come east, so they were packing up and shipping out. Rosa still lived in fear of deportation, and she knew the risks involved in starting over in a new state, but she hoped luck would be on their side. She felt luck owed them.

She didn't go into any of this with Jiminy, though she couldn't help the catch in her voice.

"I'm so sorry to hear that," Jiminy said earnestly. "You'll be missed."

Rosa bit her tongue. Hardly. But Jiminy was an exception. Rosa was aware that Jiminy was trying to take some of Fayeville's ugliness to task, and she admired her for it.

"*Gracias, amiga*," Rosa replied, as she adjusted Pen on her hip. "I'm hoping for something better for her," she continued, smoothing her baby's hair back with one hand. "I'm afraid this world isn't good enough. It's just not good enough."

Jiminy felt stricken by these words. It was only as Rosa was about to disappear through the hospital door that she found her voice again.

"Wait!" she exclaimed.

Rosa turned back, her hand still on her baby's forehead.

"I want to give you something," Jiminy declared. "It's for your daughter, really."

Rosa watched Jiminy rummage through her gigantic purse and wondered again why Americans felt the need for such large things. Big possessions, big promises, big illusions.

"Here," Jiminy said.

She was holding out a little wooden doll. Rosa could tell it was old, and exquisitely crafted. She took it gently from Jiminy's small hands and stared at it, charmed.

"It was carved to keep little girls company, when the world isn't enough," Jiminy said. "I hope your daughter will like it."

Penelope was already gripping one of the wooden arms in her little fist.

"*Muchas gracias,*" Rosa began. "Thank you. But—"

Jiminy cut her off.

"Just take care of it, please," she said. "And yourself. And your family. I'll be rooting for you."

Rosa stared a moment, then smiled for the first time in weeks.

"*Bueno,*" she said, and Jiminy felt the benediction wash over her like water.

———

Buoyed by a newfound sense of purpose, Jiminy resolved to forge ahead however possible. If she couldn't get to Travis Brayer, she'd track down Roy Tomlins. It was only as she pulled up to the small house at the end of a deserted road that she questioned the wisdom of coming alone. But she shook off her fear and approached the door with determination.

A slight, sharp-featured woman answered her knock. The right side of the woman's face was lashed with a mottled purple bruise, and there was a deep gash the length of her forehead. Jiminy couldn't help but gasp.

"What do you want?" the woman barked fiercely.

It took some effort for Jiminy to stand her ground and not step back.

"I'm looking for Roy Tomlins," she managed to respond. "Are you all right?"

"He ain't here," the woman spat. "And if I was you, I wouldn't look too hard for him. I'd run the other direction, if I was you."

Jiminy stared at her. The woman had a vein that bisected her bruise like a mountain range emerging from magma. It looked both fresh and ancient.

She slammed the door. Jiminy stood a moment, then turned and lifted her gaze to the sky. To the south, toward the river, she spotted buzzards flying high in their trademark loops. She wondered what dead or dying animal they were circling, and tried not to feel too perturbed that they seemed to be directly over Willa's farm. She straightened her shoulders and hurried toward the car.

————

From his seat beneath the hickory tree in the courthouse square, Bo watched the cars rumble past. He'd spent the morning searching for Jiminy's kitten, because he'd heard from Lyn how upset she was that it was missing. The search had been a masochistic impulse, and a fruitless one, though he was determined to resume it, despite Cole's strong objections. He wondered about his reasons as he watched the cars go by. Had the pot-holes on Main Street been filled on schedule, their rides would have been smoother, but they hadn't been fixed, so the slow-moving cars resembled lumbering animals migrating across Bo's field of vision. None of them was as tiny as the creature he was looking for.

He watched Carlos and Walton climb out of Walton's car and ascend the courthouse steps, deep in conversation. Before they reached the front door, something made them stop and turn. Bo followed their gaze and saw Rosa from Tortillas standing on the sidewalk below. Apparently she'd called to them, and now she was walking quickly toward them. Bo watched her hand over an opaque plastic bag with the Fayeville Hospital logo on it. She said something to Carlos, who listened intently before offering her his hand, which she shook before returning to her still-running car. She seemed to be in a hurry.

As she pulled back out onto the road, she narrowly missed col-liding with Roy Tomlins's truck. Roy honked and swerved, and then sped off down the uneven asphalt. Watching this, Bo felt a tingling on his arm. When he glanced down to check whether he'd been stung, he could see that he'd broken into a sweat.

———————

Roy had started drinking half an hour after he'd received word that he and Travis Brayer were persons of interest in the investi-gation of the murders of Edward and Jiminy Waters. Jean's hus-band, Floyd Butrell, had also been mentioned, but Floyd had been dead nearly as long as Edward and Jiminy, so he didn't have to weather the same indignities as those that were still around. Upon learning of the investigation, the postal service had placed Roy on leave, which freed him up for some serious drinking. At first, he'd done it to calm himself down, in the manner of strong men needing some strong stuff to fortify themselves in the face of life's setbacks. Then it had become a tribute to Travis, a string of one-man toasts to a co-conspirator and dear friend. After that, it turned into a self-pitying reflex—something to do as he cursed the existence of Carlos Castaverde and Jiminy Davis. Finally, it had become routine—Roy couldn't seem to remember a time when he hadn't been drinking, or at least he didn't want to. He preferred to define his life in whiskey terms from this point forward. Which is how he came to be ridiculously drunk outside the gate of Brayer Plantation, armed with a bottle of Jim Beam and a side of pork he planned to fry up for him and his old friend Travis.

The large wrought iron gates that framed the start of the plantation driveway hadn't been closed in decades. But they were shut now, most likely in response to the crowd of journalists camped out beyond them. Roy rolled by slowly in his truck, with his window down, marveling at the sight. One sharp-eyed local newscaster with bouffant hair caught sight of him.

"That's Roy Tomlins!" he shouted, pointing at Roy's truck.

Cameras swung in the direction of the point and microphone-wielding people began running Roy's way. Startled, Roy tried to slam his foot on the accelerator but hit the brake instead. Before he knew it, he was swarmed.

"Mr. Tomlins, did you and Travis Brayer murder Edward and Jiminy Waters?"

"Are you here to see Travis Brayer? Are you coordinating your defense?"

"Is it true you abused your job as a postal worker to spy on private citizens' correspondence?"

"What is your reaction to these murder charges?"

"Are you still active in the K.S.O.?"

Roy found the gas pedal, but his path was now completely blocked.

"Outta my way!" he yelled.

The local newscaster leaning his head inside Roy's truck winced at the whiskey smell.

"Are you intoxicated, Mr. Tomlins?" he asked.

Roy smashed the bottle of Jim Beam into the newscaster's face. The man stumbled back, blood pouring from his nose. As the surrounding crowd reacted with gasps and shouts, Roy slammed his foot on the accelerator, clipping several camera-men who didn't get out of the way fast enough, and roared down the road.

Roy felt his own blood pounding in his ears as he sped away, jerking and swerving with rage. How had this all happened? Why was everything suddenly going so wrong? It didn't make any sense to him; it wasn't supposed to be like this. This was not the way the twilight of his life was meant to unfold.

It was time to take charge. He still had some fight in him, and he wasn't going to let some uppity spic and little cunt of a girl ruin him. He'd take care of this right now.

———

Willa always left her door unlocked, and no one was able to move fast enough to rectify that situation before Roy was on the front porch, bellowing curses. Jean nearly collided with Lyn in the hall as she rushed to check on the commotion.

"What's happening?"

"Trouble," Lyn answered.

By that point, Roy was leaning into the door, determined to push it down if it didn't yield.

"Don't let him in, you hear!" Jean commanded, before hurrying into Willa's room.

Lyn didn't have a choice. She wasn't disobeying, but the door was already opening. She forced her face into a calm expression.

"Well hello, what can we do for you today, Mr. Tomplins?" Lyn tried in a friendly voice. "Mr. *Tom-lins*," she corrected herself, willing her speech impediment away. She had no time for it now.

Instead of answering, Roy shoved her roughly to the ground. She felt her back crack as she went, and wondered if she'd ever be able to convince it to work again.

"Don't you talk to me!" Roy was bellowing in her face, spewing whiskey fumes. "Don't you even look at me, you goddamn bitch!"

It had been over forty years since Roy had murdered another human being, but he remembered how it felt. He remembered the energizing thrill of surrendering to impulses. He'd also been drunk then, though not alone. He and Travis and Floyd had been together. Walton and Grady and the rest had been in other cars, too far behind to catch up in time.

Roy remembered the specific excitement of forcing Edward's car off the road, and the adrenaline rush that came with dragging a grown man somewhere he didn't want to go. He remembered the sport of letting him try to run, and how Edward had looked stumbling frantically back toward his daughter's shrieks. Roy remembered the feel of the gun against his shoulder as he'd aimed. He remembered that it had only taken one shot.

He remembered how Floyd had been spooked by the shot and let go of the girl, and that she hadn't even tried to run. She'd just knelt there on the ground, sobbing beside her father's body. Roy remembered how he had handed the gun to Travis, who'd walked over and calmly pressed its muzzle to the girl's head. Roy remembered how she'd quieted, and closed her eyes. And he remembered the hush of the night as Travis pulled the trigger.

————————

From where she lay crumpled on the floor, Lyn stayed perfectly still. She could hear Willa and Jean shrieking from the bedroom, and Roy crashing around.

Then there was the sound of tires screeching to a halt in the gravel, of running footsteps.

"NO!" Willa's granddaughter screamed from the entryway. "NO, YOU WILL NOT!"

"There you are!" Roy roared.

He'd come for the girl, Lyn realized. He'd come for the second Jiminy. Lyn couldn't let him have her. She struggled to rise.

"Don't you fucking move!" Roy snarled, as he brought his fist down hard onto Lyn's neck.

She felt something else crack, and caught a glimpse of Jiminy's horrified, terrified face as she ran toward the kitchen. Roy went after her, and though Lyn was desperate to stop him, she couldn't seem to move. Jean's gun was leaning against the wall just inside the kitchen door, but Jiminy had already run past it. Ignoring her pain, Lyn gritted her teeth and tried again to stand. But her limbs wouldn't cooperate—she was too battered and bruised. Gasping for air, with sweat pouring from her face, Lyn started to crawl.

She heard more crashes, and Jiminy screaming. With an epic effort, Lyn dragged herself through the kitchen doorway. She could see Jiminy, backed against the far counter, holding something out in front of her. But there was Roy, unstoppable, loping toward his prey. Lyn's heart began beating too fast, and there was a rushing in her ears that wasn't the sound of Roy's yelling but rather some other thing, filling her head. It was overpowering. Lyn gave herself over to it and let it move her.

Just as Roy was lunging for Jiminy, the shot rang out.

Roy lurched forward and down. Everything was silent for a long moment, and then a woman shrieked.

"Is he still alive?"

"No," Lyn heard herself reply.

And she knew it was true. Roy was dead. The rushing in Lyn's ears abruptly stopped, and she could suddenly hear the slightest noise, including the drum of a fly's wings against the kitchen window. She felt completely tapped into everything. She felt alive.

She was on her knees, with the gun still in her hands. It had only taken one shot.

"What do we do now?"

Lyn recognized this voice as Jiminy's. Roy was dead, Lyn repeated to herself. He was gone.

"I go to jail," she said matter-of-factly.

"No!" Jiminy cried.

Lyn could now see that Jiminy had been clutching the butcher knife.

"It was self-defense," Jiminy said.

"God, he's dead," Jean wailed from the doorway. "Everyone's dead. I'm so sorry, Lyn. I'm so sorry they're dead. I'm so sorry about Edward and Jiminy. I didn't know. I swear I didn't know. Floyd never said."

Jean collapsed into sobs.

"Hush now, it's over. It's all over," Lyn said soothingly, wondering at her impulse to comfort.

"But you can't go to jail for this, that's not how this ends," Jiminy protested.

Lyn stayed quiet. For several long moments, Jean's shuddering sobs were the only sound in the room. And then they stopped abruptly. Jean had mastered herself, and when she raised her head, it was evident that she'd been baptized into something new.

"Hand me the gun," she commanded.

Lyn stared at her.

"It's my gun," Jean said. "Hand it to me."

Jiminy held her breath, mesmerized.

"Are you sure?" Lyn asked Jean.

Jean nodded. She'd never been so sure of anything in her life.

THE EDITOR of the *Fayeville Ledger* couldn't explain just what exactly had happened to his town. He'd planned on a typically lazy summer. Then suddenly, everything went crazy and the entire world descended upon them. Reporters from national newspapers were camped all over, and he didn't like the way the place felt overrun. It was too much, really; he was beginning to contemplate moving someplace quieter.

In the last week alone, he'd published stories about three murders and a political suicide. Two of the murders were from over forty years ago, but the third had happened just the other day. And the political suicide came in the form of Bobby Brayer's public acknowledgment of his father's involvement in the first two murders. Bobby had withdrawn from the gubernatorial race shortly afterward, and his opponent had made a highly publicized visit to Fayeville to call for "a new era of post-racial healing." This in turn had caused a minor uproar about the use of the term "post-racial." All of these unexpected developments were linked in ways that people were still struggling to understand.

The *Ledger* was right in the middle of it. Walton Trawler had bought a whole section of the paper to publish a condensed excerpt of his latest work, which laid out exactly how the Waters murders had occurred, complete with a signed confession by Travis Brayer that named Floyd Butrell and Roy Tomlins as his accomplices.

Travis Brayer's family had initially disputed the alleged confession, claiming coercion of a seriously ill, delusional man, and the charges might have been dropped were it not for DNA evidence linking Travis to Edward Waters's burned-out car. There were rumors that someone at Fayeville Hospital had illegally provided the prosecution with hair samples from Travis Brayer to test for the match, though Carlos Castaverde refused to confirm or deny this.

The photos of Travis dressed in orange prison scrubs, wheelchair-bound and hooked up to a ventilator, had been splashed across the front pages of newspapers all over the country. Both he and Fayeville were finally famous.

In the inside section of the *Ledger,* Roy Tomlins's obituary was prominently featured. Jean Butrell had shot him, in self-defense she claimed. Everyone knew that Jean Butrell was a little crazy, but no one doubted that Roy Tomlins had had it coming. Many people were willing to testify that he'd been in a drunken rage the day he died. So though there was an investigation into the incident, most everyone assumed it was a formality and that Jean would soon be cleared.

On the page following the obituaries, Willa Hunt had taken out a full-page ad in memory of Edward and Jiminy Waters. It contained a photograph of the father and daughter when they were alive: a young Jiminy perched on Edward's shoulders, both of them smiling broadly. The photo was credited to Henry Hunt.

It wasn't the only ad space bought for them. The paper was filled with tributes—overwhelmed by them, really. All in all, the latest issue of the *Fayeville Ledger* was three times its normal thickness, and the editor was completely exhausted.

———

Jiminy was sitting on the stool in Willa's kitchen, glancing through this issue as she sorted the silverware Willa had decided to donate to Goodwill, when Bo turned into the driveway. She didn't see him at first. Neither did Carlos, who was sipping coffee by the sink as he contemplated Jiminy's profile, wondering whether she could sustain his interest.

No one had gone into Willa's kitchen for days after the police had removed Roy's body, until Willa had asked Jiminy to reclaim the space for the living. Jiminy, in turn, had recruited Carlos to join her in the reclamation project. She preferred being with Carlos to being alone. He was flawed, but fascinating, and Jiminy suspected that for the first time, she enjoyed the upper hand. This intrigued her.

"Did you like Texarkana when you visited?" Carlos asked her, apropos of nothing.

"I didn't do much touring," Jiminy replied without looking up. "I stopped at your office and at Sonic for some onion rings, and that was pretty much it."

"I think you should come back with me," Carlos announced. "Or wherever I go next, maybe you should come along. We make a good team."

It was true that they did. Jiminy knew he was referring to more than their ability to solve cold case crimes, and it was a tempting offer. But even if Bo hadn't been directly in Jiminy's line of sight when she looked up from the paper, she still would have known she had to turn Carlos down. Because before she'd even looked up, just as soon as Carlos had finished his sentence, something inside her had shouted no. She'd heard it clearly—felt it, really, like a gong vibration in her chest. It was deep, resonant, and absolutely definitive. All that Carlos was offering was extremely interesting, but it wasn't for her.

On top of which, there was Bo through the freshly cleaned window, walking toward the front door, carrying Cholera with him.

"I can't," Jiminy said.

She should have at least looked at Carlos when she said it, but her eyes were locked on Bo. Carlos followed her gaze, then put his coffee cup down.

The sound of it against the countertop snapped Jiminy back into herself. She blinked and turned to Carlos.

"I'm sorry," she said. "I am. But the thing is," she continued, pointing as she moved to open the door, "that's my cat."

My father used to tell me that there's only so much space inside a person, so you have to be careful what you let fill you up. Anger and bitterness and despair will crowd in if you let them, he said, but so will mercy and forgiveness and joy—if you make the room and invite them in. Sometimes you have to work extra hard to make the room.

His Manual for Life advice, he called it.

It's funny that I'm thinking about it now.

It's funny that you can't really understand the best way to do a thing until after it's done. But good advice is good advice, and good advice is never too late, even when it seems like it is.

I consider Edward my father, by the way. I liked Henry very much, but I loved Edward. I had two fathers, I guess.

We were a family, as damaged and strange as any of them.

I know my mother misses us. I visit her often. I was with her when she shot Roy, and I'm watching her now.

Lyn is standing on the riverbank, staring into the water. I know she's thinking of me because I can feel her as clearly as I used to feel my own thoughts spearing through my brain. She's wondering if I've stayed the same age, if I'm happy, if she'll see me again. I have, I am, and she will. I beam these answers to her as best I can, in little flashes of silver, and I hope that the way she just pressed her hand into her chest means that she understands.

She's suffered so much.

She's unbuttoning her blouse now, and slipping her arms out of it. She's carefully stepping out of her long skirt. Everything she does is very slow and deliberate, in time with her rhythmic breathing. It's ritualistic, exactly as she intends it.

The only noise is the sound of the crickets starting up. She can hear them all around her. I know she thinks it's a way that I talk to her. Maybe it is.

She's out of her slip and her bra, and she's taken the pins from her hair. She's even unwrapped the bandage from her head. Everything is discarded on the bank.

With slow, careful steps, she makes her way down to the water and wades in. I know how cold the river is, but she doesn't hesitate. She keeps walking, letting the water seep up over her knees and her hips and the lower back that gives her so much pain. It's above her waist now, and her elbows, and now her breasts. When it comes up to her chin, she stops and sinks down underwater, where she stays for as long as she can. For as long as a human can. She weighs herself down with all her unfulfilled years, gripping roots to hold herself tight to the bottom. I can feel the last traces of oxygen leaving her lungs, abandoning her body, releasing outward.

But when she surges back up into the late summer air, she's not gasping.

She's free.